SCREAMING
QUIETLY

evan jacobs

SADDLEBACK
PUBLISHING

GRAVEL ROAD

Bi-Normal
Edge of Ready
Falling Out of Place
Screaming Quietly
2 Days
Unchained

SADDLEBACK
P U B L I S H I N G
www.sdlback.com

ISBN-13: 978-1-62250-003-1
ISBN-10: 1-62250-003-2
eBook: 978-1-61247-687-2

Printed in Guangzhou, China
NOR/0313/CA21300400

17 16 15 14 13   1 2 3 4 5

Sometimes we find ourselves on a gravel road, not sure of how we got there or where the road leads. Sharp stones pellet the unprotected. And the everyday wear and tear sears more deeply.

Dedication

For my father, Sidney and my mother, Ronni. Andrew and I will surely see you again. This book is inspired by all the students I am lucky enough to work with every day. For Tyler F ... your penchant for not wanting to read led me to this publisher! And of course ... for Shawn.

CHAPTER 1

Practice

Ian didn't think it was possible to sweat more that afternoon. Football practice had worn him out. He was just happy it was Friday. The end of hell week. Then school started the following Thursday.

This would be Ian's first year playing as a wide receiver for Davis High School. He had been at the school since last fall but arrived too late to play.

At his old school when he was a freshman, Ian had a reputation as one of the best frosh-soph football players. Of course Coach Banks and Coach Geary, the varsity and junior varsity coaches, didn't let Ian know they knew this. They just threw him in with the JV team. Ian could see they were impressed. Especially when he met all of their challenges. Whether it was testing his speed, endurance, or ability to pick the right moves to make, Ian never seemed phased. He never seemed rattled.

For Ian Taylor the grueling activity of the football field was a welcome change from the chaos of his life.

Practice was winding down.

As much as Ian had sweat, as much as he had run, as much energy as he'd used up, he still felt pretty good. All the other players had their mouths open. They looked exhausted. Something about this always inspired Ian. It made him try harder. He was still sweating a lot, but none of that seemed to matter. He was in a zone. Everybody was waiting for practice to be over. Ian was waiting for the next play. He didn't care that this was just his team playing against itself in a scrimmage.

"You play how you practice," Ian told himself.

Everybody wearily took their spots in the formation. Ian was already at his. He stood at the ready, his muscles tensing, ready to take off across the field.

"Hike," the quarterback called. The ball was in play.

Ian moved across the field as if practice had just started. He could almost feel Coach Geary, the JV cheerleaders, and some of the people in the bleachers watching him. He moved to the area of the field where the least amount of players were. Ian quickly whipped around. The pass traveled through the air. It was as if the quarterback had been waiting for Ian to catch it.

Ian had always been a good judge of where the ball was going to land. He saw the other players on the team moving toward him. Ian began moving again. The ball glided into his hands. It was so effortlessly done that Ian didn't really even feel it land. Before he knew it, he had run under the goal post, leaving the other players who sought to tackle him behind by many yards.

It may as well have been miles.

"Good scrimmage, Taylor. Great field instincts. Great hustle," Coach Geary said as Ian walked with some of his teammates toward the showers. Everyone seemed to be hobbling along. Ian had a lot of spring in his step.

When he got to his locker, he checked his cell phone.

His mom had called. He'd call her later.

Jessica Barnes had texted him. "What r u doing tonight?" she asked.

He'd have to think about that and text her back. As was usually the case with Ian Taylor, he had to think before making his next move.

Even the small ones.

CHAPTER 2

Evasion Tactics

Come on, Ian ..." Shawn went on. "You never hang out."

"I do to," Ian said. Ian, Shawn, and Ryan were walking across the school's practice field. "I just can't today."

"We barely saw you at all this summer," Ryan offered.

Ian was used to hearing this. He never hung out. He never went to parties. He rarely did anything with his friends.

Then Ian remembered that he still needed to call his mom and return Jessica's text.

"I'm doing something with Jessica,"

he said. The guys couldn't give him any grief about that. Jessica was a girl. What high school boy wouldn't ditch his friends to hang out with a girl? Especially Jessica Barnes. She had flowing blonde hair and a perfect complexion. Jessica had eyes that seemed to scoop you up, willingly or otherwise, whenever you looked into them.

"Oh, that's right," Shawn said, his tone softening. "You guys have been hanging out."

"Yeah," Ian said. They hadn't been hanging out that much, but he wasn't going to tell Shawn or Ryan that. "Maybe we can go to the movies tomorrow?"

Shawn shrugged.

"With Jessica?" Ryan asked. He was unable to hide his excitement.

"No," Ian said. "Just us."

"Ahhh ... I was hoping she could bring some friends."

Ian walked with them for a little while longer, then cut out.

The master of evasion had struck again.

Ian was going to text Jessica. But first he had to call his mom. She probably wanted to make sure he was going to be home to take care of his brother, Davey. The brother that nobody knew he had. At this school anyway.

It hadn't been that bad when Davey was younger. All of Ian's friends seemed to accept that his brother was "different." And they mostly ignored him. But as Davey got older, he became harder for everybody to ignore. That's when Ian started keeping secrets.

Davey's autism was all that Ian's mom talked about back then. Ian had heard his mom talk about it so many times that he couldn't even pinpoint when he knew his brother had autism.

By the time Davey was in kindergarten, he was known for being a tough kid. He wasn't tough in a talk back, disrespectful kind of way. He just got frustrated by the simplest things. When this happened, it didn't matter where he was, it didn't matter who was around him. Davey would go off.

He'd bite others or himself, kick, scream, cry, pull hair, and scratch. A lot of the time Ian, his mom, and his dad (before his parents got divorced) would have no idea what the problem was or how to calm him down.

This was stuff Ian had heard about or witnessed. He could only imagine the stuff Davey had done that his parents hadn't told him about. When his dad lived at home, his parents would argue about Davey and what he had done on a particular day. It seemed like they were constantly arguing.

Back then Ian always knew when Davey had a problem in school because one of his parents' cars would be in the driveway when he got home. A lot of times, if he was having a tantrum about something, Ian would hear Davey screaming as he approached the house. A few times Ian had friends with him. As soon as he'd hear those all-too-familiar shrieks, Ian knew he had to act quickly. He'd tell a potential guest he had chores to do. He'd forgotten about them. He couldn't hang out any longer. Or he'd say they had to go somewhere else because he just remembered his parents didn't want anybody over that day.

Anything.

Anything he could think of to get out of that situation and keep Davey a secret. The neighbors knew about him. A lot of people knew at the first house they lived in. But after the divorce, Ian, his mom, and

Davey moved. The only people who knew about him now—about his brother with autism—were family and the neighbors. After the move, Ian stopped having friends come over.

Davey needed to be in a special class: an autism-specific class with people like him. Ian's schools had never had a class like that. Ian was safe. Safe in his world. As long as he didn't let anybody in, how would anybody find out that there was a kid like Davey in the Taylor house?

Ian called his mom. She worked as a sales rep at a medical supply company. He usually got her voicemail when he called. When her familiar message came on, Ian hung up the phone. If she wanted him for anything, it was probably for Davey. And Ian was on his way home anyway.

CHAPTER 3

Davey

Ian walked into the house to the sounds of Davey bouncing on a big plastic sensory ball in the living room. The whole house, except for Ian's bedroom, seemed to be set up for Davey. There were three bedrooms, but the living room was the center of all activity. Due to autism, Davey was constantly "seeking sensory input" as Ian's mom said.

The living room was littered with squeeze toys that Davey loved to use. Ian noticed how hard Davey grabbed them. It looked like he was going to crush them into oblivion. There was also a small trampoline, which Davey liked to jump on. Ian went on it a little bit when he was younger, but when he realized it was for Davey—and why it was for him—Ian wanted nothing to do with it. The last thing he wanted was for anybody to think that he was "like" his brother.

The living room also had weighted blankets Davey loved to lie under. They weren't big. They reminded Ian of the kind of vest you wore when you were having an x-ray at the dentist. There was something about the pressure of them that calmed Davey down. On the table in the living room was a slant board. It looked like a large, three-ring binder, only it was sturdier. Paper could be clipped at the top of the slope so Davey could write on it. The board helped because it meant he didn't have to put so much pressure on the paper to write. Davey may have been able to squeeze hard, but he had trouble holding small objects.

There were also a lot of DVDs. Davey really loved movies. Many of them were for much younger kids, but Davey didn't care. He would just as soon watch *Thomas & Friends* and *Finding Nemo* as he would *The Suite Life of Zach & Cody*. Davey played a lot with dolls and stuffed animals. He didn't care that he was fourteen years old and was supposed to be into cooler stuff.

Ian heard Greg Bowers, Davey's aide at school and at home, working with him in the living room. They did this thing called ABA. It stood for Applied Behavior Analysis. Ian didn't understand it. To him it was just Greg asking Davey a lot of the same questions, then Greg would write down Davey's responses or actions in a binder. One thing it did do was help Davey communicate. When he was younger, he didn't talk. So he got mad. A lot. Once he started doing ABA, he didn't get mad as much because he could finally say what he wanted or describe how he was feeling.

Ian liked Greg. He was a big guy. Strong. He could handle Davey with one hand. He was cool too. He wore cool clothes, and he had cool short hair and a goatee. Davey listened to him. Greg saw to it that Davey stayed in line at school. Davey still might throw a tantrum with Greg. But Greg was always calm, and there was never any fear that Davey would overpower him.

When Greg wasn't there—when it was just Ian and his mom—that's when Ian had to be the man of the house. He could usually handle things, but if Davey was really upset—if he was screaming, crying, and trying to destroy everything in his path— both of them had to work together to calm Davey down. Ian hated seeing his mother attacked. He loved his brother, but sometimes he wished Davey wasn't around.

"How was practice?" Greg asked, giving Ian a high five. Greg had played football in high school. He was twenty-eight now.

"It was good. Hot," Ian said.

"Hell week." Greg nodded.

"It sucked," Ian said.

"You start school next week?"

"Yeah, Thursday."

"Enjoy it, Ian. You're playing for a good school."

Davey came over and wrapped his arms around Greg. This was his way of showing Greg that he was happy to have him over that day. To anybody else this would have looked weird. Davey was fourteen, but he was actually bigger than Ian. Since he didn't exercise, he was out of shape. Even though Greg was much bigger than Davey, Davey still had the element of surprise going for him.

"What do you want, Davey?" Greg asked playfully. He started giving him squeezes all over his arms. He tickled his belly. Davey's eyes were wide, and his mouth hung open in a smile.

"Ian," Davey said as he turned and put his arms around him now. Ian gave Davey a hug.

"Hey, Davey," Ian said.

Greg's cell phone rang. He looked at it.

"I gotta get this. Be right back." Greg walked out of the room.

Ian squeezed and tickled Davey for a while. Davey loved it and laughed. Then his demeanor changed slightly.

"Video. Movie," Davey said.

He used his size and pushed Ian to the ground. Davey took the TV remote and turned on a *SpongeBob SquarePants* DVD.

The minute it started, Davey squeezed his hands into fists and gritted his teeth.

"Breathe, Davey," Ian reminded him. Their mom had pointed out that when Davey got excited like this, he sometimes held his breath. "Or we'll have to turn the video off."

"No video off," Davey said. He looked at Ian very seriously. He wasn't angry. Not yet. Davey was scared he was going to lose his video.

"Then breathe," Ian said.

Davey watched the video. Then he started to laugh. He hit the floor with his hands. He squeezed Ian. Davey kicked out his legs. He slapped them with his hands and pulled on his shorts. All of this showed how much he was enjoying watching the DVD. Everything he liked, he seemed to like more than everybody else. He would stare at the TV, as if in a trance, and lose himself in whatever he was watching. Ian had never seen anybody enjoy cartoons or movies the way Davey enjoyed them.

Even if he had seen it a million times, Davey's reactions never changed. Davey never changed.

CHAPTER 4

Mom

Ian's mom, Melissa, came in the house but didn't shut the door.

"You guys ready to go eat?" she called.

Ian was online looking over the classes he could take as a sophomore. He was stoked that he could take driver's education. The only problem was that a letter had gone out saying that the class was impacted. Apparently, due to where Ian's last name fell in the alphabet, he would have to wait until next semester.

"McDonald's," Davey said as Ian heard him walk out and greet his mom.

He could also hear Davey wrap his arms around her. Ian loved his mom, but he didn't worry if she was going to come home or not. Davey had a lot of anxiety when she wasn't around. Davey always had a written schedule he could refer to no matter who was watching him. It always ended, "And when I leave, Mom comes home."

"I'm gonna stay here," Ian called out. He didn't look up from the computer in his sparsely furnished bedroom. There was a bed (which he was lying on), a dresser, a small table for him to do his homework, a TV, and his laptop. He didn't have anything on the walls.

"Well," Melissa started, "it looks like it's just you and me tonight, Davey."

She gave him a kiss.

"Ian," Davey said.

Ian closed his eyes. Now he would get the guilt trip. Not from his mom but from

Davey. His mom wasn't trying to be mean. She wasn't trying to keep Ian from having a life of his own. But that's how he felt. She always seemed to let Davey win.

He wanted to scream, "Why can't I just do what I want?" quietly, so as not to disturb the neighbors.

But he didn't. Ian never really showed his emotions.

"Well, go tell him," Melissa said to Davey.

Ian could hear the sound of their footsteps moving over the carpet. Then they were in his doorway. Davey walked into Ian's bedroom.

"Okay, everybody," Davey said, repeating the way he had heard people ask others to do things. "It's time to go to McDonald's."

When Davey talked, it was often hard to know what he was saying. Unless you spoke "Davey." Even though what he said was labored, *he* knew what he was trying to say. Then there were times, like now when he asked Ian to come to dinner, he could say the words perfectly because he had said them so many times before.

Ian looked at his mom. He wanted to help. But he also wanted to work on his school schedule. And to call Jessica after that. He wanted his mom to tell Davey, "No. Ian wants to stay home." She was strict with Davey about some things. But not about letting him have access to Ian. Sometimes Ian wondered if his mom ever thought about how he might just want to be alone. She didn't seem to care.

"Sounds like he really wants you to go." Melissa smiled. She looked tired. She worked forty hours a week. Sometimes more. Ian thought that the stress of managing Davey was aging her. He didn't know if his mom was pretty. But she'd had a lot of boyfriends since the divorce.

"They must think she's good looking," he thought. "Okay," Ian sighed. He closed his laptop and got off the bed.

Davey was already walking out of the room.

There was more traffic than usual on the road tonight.

"Everybody was running after me, but they couldn't get me. I knew they couldn't," Ian said excitedly as he recounted football practice to his mom. She was driving with a Bluetooth receiver in her ear.

"That's great, sweetie." Melissa had her eyes on the car in front of them, as well as on Davey in the rearview mirror.

He was playing with a Bambi doll and some other action figures from Disney cartoons. Ian thought he sounded happy because he was making a lot of noise. They were short, quick noises, and Davey usually gritted his teeth when he did that. It meant he was excited.

"You think you're the best player on the team?" his mom asked. She looked at him now. Ian didn't know if she was being serious or if she was teasing him because he'd been bragging. "It sounds like you are."

"I don't know ..." Ian said. He thought he was the best player on the junior varsity team, but he felt weird saying it.

Melissa's phone rang.

She looked at it. Before Ian could answer her question, she said, "Hello."

By the way she spoke—her voice had a nervous excitement about it—Ian knew she was talking to her boyfriend, Todd. They had been dating for about two months. Ian thought he was okay. He tried too hard to make Ian and Davey like him. He would say things he thought were cool. He'd buy Ian football-related things he didn't ask for, and he'd go out of his way to play with Davey. A few times he had crowded Davey so much that he actually set him off. Ian ended up having to calm Davey down.

"Do you really like Todd?" Ian imagined asking his mom. "Or are you just lonely?" Ian didn't understand why his parents couldn't suck it up and stay together. If not for themselves, then for him and Davey. But his dad had moved on with someone else too.

As Melissa talked with Todd, Ian knew his conversation with her was over. It usually happened like this. His mom would give him her attention for a little while. But once Davey, a guy, or one of her friends called, Ian was forgotten.

Ian didn't dwell on this too long. He took out his phone and saw the text from Jessica. It had been hours since she'd sent it.

"Sorry I didn't txt sooner. How are you?" Ian quickly wrote. At first Jessica didn't respond. Ian wondered if she was mad he'd taken so long to get back to her. It would be just his luck. He got one of the best-looking cheerleaders at Davis High School to date him, and he blew it because he didn't text her back in time.

Ian had started playing a football app on his phone when she replied.

"Im good. What r u doing?"

"Eating with my mom. U?"

"About to eat too. Wanna hang out after?" she asked.

She asked him to hang out. Ian could feel himself getting excited. He liked Jessica a lot. He wasn't totally relaxed around her, but he figured that was because he liked her so much.

"Sure. Ill come over around 9," Ian wrote. He was going to put a question mark at the end of that text, but he had always been told that girls liked it if a guy took charge.

"K. Cant wait 2 C U!" Jessica wrote back.

Ian stared at his phone, and for the moment, he didn't have a problem in the world.

Meltdown

Ian loved his mom, but she often frustrated him. Sometimes she was really on the ball, and other times it was like she was still in high school.

Melissa had been on the phone with Todd when she ordered the food. Big mistake. She ordered all the food at once. This included Davey's chocolate sundae. Normally Ian's mom ordered the food she wanted Davey to eat, and then she went back and ordered him his dessert. This way Davey had to eat his dinner if he wanted his mom to buy the sundae.

She didn't do that tonight. So while she talked with Todd on the phone, Ian watched as Davey took a few bites of his hamburger (normally he had to eat the whole thing), ate a few fries, and then eyed his melting ice-cream sundae.

Ian did what he always did whenever they were out in public. He looked around to see if there was anybody he recognized. He knew he couldn't keep everybody from knowing about Davey forever. But if he consciously avoided situations where he could potentially bump into friends, the chance of anybody finding out was that much less. Ian didn't see anybody he knew at McDonald's.

Then he noted how many people were in the restaurant. Not many.

Lastly, he realized that he instinctively had them sit close to the door. He always tried to do this when he was out with Davey. If he got upset, Ian and his mom could take him out of wherever they were so they wouldn't ruin other people's meals.

"Sundae," Davey said softly.

"Finish your food, Davey." Ian's mom was still on the phone.

Now Davey was starting to get mad.

Nobody would know it to look at Ian, but his insides were getting tense.

"Sundae!" Davey exclaimed. Ian was happy Davey didn't scream, but it was loud enough to turn a few heads in the restaurant. Ian was already going into that mode where he pretended like he didn't hear people talking.

"Three more bites, Davey," Ian said calmly. Sometimes, if somebody other than the person who wanted Davey to do something asked, Davey would do it. A lot of people thought Davey wasn't smart. He might not be IQ smart, but Ian figured he had to be pretty intelligent to be that stubborn.

For a moment Ian thought it had worked. Davey picked up his hamburger, never taking his eyes off the sundae, and put it in his mouth. But instead of taking a bite, he put the hamburger back on the table.

"No more," Davey whined. He still wasn't getting loud. Just angry.

"Davey," Ian stated sternly. "You're not gonna get your sundae if you don't eat your food."

Personally, Ian would've given him the sundae just to avoid him getting upset. But Melissa didn't allow it. They had to be strict with their demands, otherwise Davey wouldn't learn.

"NO MORE FOOD!" Davey yelled.

He tried to reach for the sundae. His mom, finally realizing that she had messed up buying it with the meal, moved it out of the way.

"I WANT ICE CREAM!" Davey screeched.

Ian didn't have to look around the restaurant. He knew that everybody was watching them. And that's all they would do. Nobody ever tried to get involved. That was one thing Ian was thankful for.

"Davey!" Melissa was trying to remain composed. "I'll give you the sundae after you calm down and finish your food."

And then, as if he couldn't control himself, Davey hit Ian's mom on the shoulder. Ian didn't react. In a way he felt his mom deserved it. She shouldn't have been on the phone. She should have been thinking when she ordered the food.

"This never would have happened if Dad was here," he thought. And that made him even angrier and more embarrassed.

"Mad!" Davey yelled. He had been taught to express his feelings when he was angry. Sometimes this helped if he was about to have a meltdown, but it was useless when he was already having one.

"Davey, settle down," Melissa said firmly. Ian knew that wasn't going to work.

Davey grabbed his mom's hair. This time Ian sprang into action. He tried to unhook Davey's hand without hurting his mom.

"Ice cream!" Davey yelled again.

He let go of Melissa's hair and stood up. He lunged for the ice cream. Ian blocked him and got to his feet. Davey tried to push him. Ian grabbed his hand. Davey tried to hit him with the other one. Ian grabbed that as well.

Then, with all of his strength, Ian moved Davey out of McDonald's. They passed a family with three little kids. Ian pushed Davey faster because he knew if he didn't, Davey would try and kick one of them. Ian had heard that some people with autism only get upset at the person who's making them angry. Not Davey. He would go after anybody he could get his hands on.

Ian got Davey on the grass in front of McDonald's and dropped him there. He stood back as Davey had a tantrum on the ground. He put enough distance between him and Davey so that if Davey got up and went after him, Ian could stop him. He also maneuvered himself so that if Davey made a run for the street or the restaurant, he could stop him.

Melissa walked outside. Ian looked at her and then at Davey. He had been too quick to get Davey out of there. In his haste, he had placed Davey squarely in front of the window where everybody was eating.

McDonald's patrons were all getting a front row view of Davey Taylor having a classic meltdown.

CHAPTER 6

Aftermath

As quickly as Davey had gotten mad, it seemed like he calmed down. Ian was sitting in the front seat pretending to play *Tank Hero* on his phone. Melissa was back on the phone with Todd, finishing up her conversation. Davey, as if he'd never been mad at all, sat in the back seat playing with his toys. Now he was making noises that sounded like a conversation, but he was most likely reciting lines from one of his favorite shows or movies. This seemed to help center Davey. It kept him calm.

Melissa got off the phone.

"Ian," his mom started, "I don't know what I would do without you."

"You shouldn't have ordered the sundae until after he'd eaten." Ian didn't look up from his game when he said that. He hoped his mom would know he was mad. That Davey had embarrassed both of them for the umpteenth time, and it was her fault.

"Yeah, I was on the phone. I wasn't thinking."

"I'll say," Ian wanted to add. But he didn't. He didn't want to be mean to his mom. He loved her. She was a strong woman. She did a lot for him and Davey. She had stuck around after their father left.

"Anyway, I mean it, Ian." She ran her hand through his hair. "I don't know what I would do without you."

Ian wondered what she would do without him too. He wasn't going to live at home forever. He wanted to get into a good college. Play football there ... maybe on a scholarship. Get as far away from Davey as possible ... but could he? Could he really leave them?

"Thanks." Ian smiled at his mom.

Normally, they might have had a longer conversation, but Ian didn't want to. They were almost home, and Ian wanted to see Jessica. He'd given up enough of his night already.

CHAPTER 7

Jessica

Ian's heart raced a bit as Jessica opened
the door and met him on the front porch of
her parents' house. Ian lived in a one-story
home that his mom rented. Jessica lived in
a large two-story home that Ian figured her
parents owned.

It was a warm summer night, and
Jessica had her long blonde hair pulled
back. She wore a tight T-shirt and a pair of
curve-hugging shorts. She looked perfect
to Ian. In his mind it was effortless for her
to be that way. He always felt he looked
average. He had short blonde hair and
mostly wore jeans and T-shirts. His clothes

were old. His mom hadn't done his and Davey's back-to-school shopping yet.

"I'm glad you finally texted me back." Jessica smiled.

They started walking down the street. He figured they would make their way over to the park near her house. They'd been there a few times together. That's where they'd first kissed. They hadn't done much more than that, but Ian was okay with it. He figured if things kept going well, they would.

"I heard about the team scrimmage today," Jessica said. She wrapped her arm around Ian's as they walked. He smiled because he thought they probably looked like an old married couple. He thought Jessica liked him a lot. And he sure liked her, even though they didn't really know each other. Even after a month of dating.

"How'd you hear about that?" Ian asked. Jessica was a junior, and she was on the varsity cheerleading team. All the cheerleaders practiced when their specific team (varsity, junior varsity, frosh-soph) practiced.

"Amanda Brown. She told me nobody can believe how fast you are." Amanda was a cheerleader on the junior varsity squad.

"I'm just lucky, I guess." Ian didn't know how to respond to compliments. He didn't know what to say back. It probably had something to do with not knowing how to take them. Or maybe he didn't get them enough to understand what they were.

He was going to have to figure out how to fit Jessica into his life more. He loved being around her. He felt like he *needed* to be around Jessica. As if she, the football team, and everybody else who didn't know about his brother made him more normal.

"Everybody says you're really good. You'll definitely be on varsity when you're a junior." Jessica leaned herself into him a little bit as they walked. They were almost at the park. "Then I can cheer just for you."

"When I make a touchdown, I'll be sure to point at you every time." He felt dumb after he said that. Jessica just smiled.

Ian could talk about school, football, and even cheer with Jessica. However, he couldn't really share anything else with her. He didn't want to. He wasn't ready for that. Maybe someday. If he got more comfortable around her.

The only problem for Ian was that it wasn't just Jessica. It was everybody else who was wrapped up in their lives. Since it was summer, Ian only saw the junior varsity players and the cheerleaders. Once school started, everybody would be together. Including Steve Morgan, Jessica's old boyfriend. Making matters worse,

Steve played Ian's position on the varsity squad. He ignored the comments people made that Jessica "only went for those kinda guys."

They continued talking when they got to the park. Ian talked about some guys on the JV team. Jessica talked about some of the cheerleaders. How catty and bitchy they could be. Then, somehow, they ended up kissing.

Ian was never sure how it happened, but he was always glad when it did. He wondered if this was what "being smooth" was. If he just naturally had the ability to make things like this happen to make girls like him.

Jessica's lips were really soft. She was really soft. She smelled so good to Ian. So fresh. So free. He wondered how he smelled to her.

He didn't want to ask. Ian was afraid of the answer.

Varsity

Ian Taylor?" the manager of the varsity team asked. His name was Scott Perez. Ian had never spoken to him before. He just knew who he was because Ian always saw him walking with Coach Banks, the varsity coach.

"Yeah," Ian said. Practice had just started on Monday morning, but Coach Geary didn't have them running any plays yet. The team was just stretching.

"Coach Banks wants you to come to his office."

Ian looked at Shawn, who was standing next to him.

"Okay, I'm gonna tell Coach Geary."

"It's okay. Coach Geary knows," Scott responded.

Ian followed Scott off the field.

"I haven't seen anybody move like you on the field since this school was built in the 1970s," Coach Banks said. Ian didn't know how old Coach Banks was, but he figured if he'd been coaching at Davis since the 1970s, he must be ancient.

His office was filled with pictures from football games, practices, random coaching events. There were also a bunch of trophies, two CIF Championships, plaques, etc.

"You've got good instincts. You just seem to know what you're doing out there. Most importantly, you're relaxed. You're comfortable." Coach Banks stared at Ian. He had a gleam in his eye, as if he was seeing Ian in the future. Seeing how great Ian could be for the Davis football team.

"Thanks," Ian said. He was always one of the top three players on any team he played on. But nobody had ever really talked to him that way about football before. Ian felt as if Coach Banks had been researching him. Breaking down his game so he could make it better ... but why?

"I love playing football, sir," Ian added.

"And it shows." Coach Banks sat up in his chair. He moved closer to Ian across his desk, which was covered with papers. "How'd you like to be on the varsity squad this year?"

Ian couldn't believe what he just heard.

"We don't usually have sophomores on our squad, but I want to make an exception in your case."

"Okay ... but what about Steve Morgan? Is he gonna play a different position?" Ian was so excited he was having trouble putting his words together. He wondered briefly if maybe this was how Davey felt when he was trying to say something.

"Well, I'm not gonna BS you, Ian. Steve is a senior, you're a sophomore, so he'll probably play a lot more than you. But—and this stays between us—Steve has some things he needs to deal with. That might keep him from playing certain games. That's when I'd use you to fill his spot."

What kind of things could Steve Morgan have to deal with? Was he sick or something? He was only two years older than Ian.

"So whaddya say?" Coach Banks extended his hand. "Are you up for it? You ready to be a varsity man?"

"Yeah, sure. Of course," Ian said. He shook Coach Banks's enormous hand. It was so big and rough that it seemed to swallow Ian's fingers.

"Well, congratulations, Ian. You're gonna be a varsity man for the rest of your high school career."

As Ian went back to practice, he couldn't believe what had just happened. He knew he was good at football, but he didn't think he would get promoted so soon. Ian wasn't small, but he wasn't big either. Some of those varsity players were giants. He knew that his opponents would target the smallest players on the team. And that meant him, a lowly sophomore who was suddenly playing with the big boys.

Ian wasn't going to think about any of that now.

With Davey around, Ian rarely ever got any attention at home. He'd gotten some awards his freshman year at his old school for being a good player. But those didn't count. Nobody really cared about the freshman games.

He got attention for playing football when he was younger, even from his parents—the people who really mattered. But now his dad usually couldn't make his games because he lived too far away. His mom, when she was there, was always cheering for him. However, more often than not, she had to leave the game early because she was with Davey, who was "over" being there. When that happened, Ian would get a ride home with one of the other players on the team. Their parents usually told Ian how great he did. They even took him out sometimes.

But it wasn't the same as having his parents there.

With the promotion to varsity, Ian hoped his parents couldn't help but take notice of him. Davis High School might really be his place to shine.

CHAPTER 9

Celebration Hang

I'm sorta bummed, but I'm also stoked for you at the same time," Ryan said.

Ian, Shawn, and Ryan had gone out for pizza at the mall after practice. Ian didn't have to be home until later that afternoon when he'd have to be around to help his mom with Davey. He was really thankful when he found out that varsity practice started right after junior varsity, as that would still give him some free time … until school started on Thursday.

His mom had set up a schedule with various neighbors so that Davey had somebody watching him until she came home. Ian wasn't expected to be home when the neighbors were there, but they sure seemed to appreciate it when he was. Ian felt he had more freedom when Greg was there working with Davey. He was only in the house two hours, three times a week, though.

It seemed to Ian that his mom sort of assumed that if she was home with Davey, Ian would be there too. Ian thought she probably figured that going to school and practice was enough of a social life for him.

"Yeah," Shawn said, continuing Ryan's thought about Ian being on varsity now. Ian had to admit that he liked all the attention this was getting him so far. "It's like, I know we'll play together on varsity in a year or two. I just wish we could still play together now."

"Yeah, I know. But we're all playing for Davis even though we're on different teams." Ian grabbed another slice of the pepperoni pizza they had bought at the food court.

"JV won't be the same without you. They're probably gonna put Gerald Golub in your spot. He sucks," Shawn stated.

Ian wanted to tell Shawn it wouldn't be *that* bad, but he couldn't. Gerald sucked at football.

"Oh man," Ryan half screamed. "I didn't even think about that. Our team is gonna be awful."

All three of them laughed.

Just then, one of the workers in the food court moved past the three of them. He didn't seem to notice the boys at all. The worker started cleaning the table next to theirs. Whoever had been there had left all their trash.

The worker's movements were jerky, as if half of his body didn't work. He also seemed to favor his left hand over his right. He acted like someone Ian had seen before ... at one of the therapy centers Davey had gone to years ago. His mom had told him the person had cerebral palsy.

The man was trying to push all of the trash into a bag. He tried to do too much of it and a piece fell on the floor. He bent down and awkwardly picked it up.

Shawn laughed a little. Ryan did as well but then kicked Shawn for laughing at someone with a disability.

Ian looked at them. He wanted to tell them that this person had special needs. That they were stupid for laughing at him. That if they were making fun of him, then they were making fun of his brother. He had no doubt in his mind that these guys would make fun of Davey.

But Ian didn't say anything. He never did.

And when the worker with cerebral palsy was far enough away, Ian laughed with his friends.

CHAPTER 10

Absent Father

Ian was watching *TRON: Legacy* with Davey—one of the few age-appropriate movies that Davey liked—when the phone rang. He heard his mom pick it up, and a few minutes later she came into the room with the phone. She handed it to Ian.

"It's your dad. I want you to tell him the big news yourself," she said. Melissa walked out of the room. She was still upset at their father for leaving them. She wanted nothing to do with him.

"Hey, Dad," Ian said.

"Hey, buddy," Ian's dad sounded like he was driving around in Los Angeles traffic. "So what's this news you want to tell me?"

Ian then heard the receiver muffle. Like his dad was telling somebody something he didn't want him to hear.

"I made varsity my sophomore year." Ian wanted to be more excited when he told him. It was just hard because Ian knew his dad wasn't really paying attention.

"Really? That's great, Ian! You're a great player." The phone muffled again. Then his dad came back. "Varsity, huh?"

"Yeah. The coach says I'll be a varsity player for the rest of the time that I'm ..." Ian heard the receiver muffle again. His dad wasn't even listening to him now. He was probably with his girlfriend, Amy. The woman he was going to marry. She would be Ian's stepmom.

There was a pause. Ian's dad was still talking with whoever he was with. Eventually, he came back.

"I'm really proud of you, Ian. Varsity. That's great."

Ian could've told him anything, and his dad would've said that.

"Davey and I are gonna be there this weekend." Ian hoped this would get his dad interested. They always visited their father the first weekend school started. The tradition started the first year he'd left their mom. They were supposed to visit him every other weekend of the month but that didn't always happen.

Davey looked over at Ian when he said that. They stared at each other. This always surprised Ian. You could be talking to Davey and he wouldn't answer you. A lot of the time he wouldn't even look in your direction. Then there were times you'd be talking and he'd hear something and get involved in the conversation. Maybe that was what autism was: if you didn't care, you didn't care, but when you cared, you *really* cared.

"Yeah, Ian, about that ..." his dad started.

Ian's heart sank. Davey was still looking at him. Ian immediately knew this was going to be a problem.

"Amy and I have a lot to do this weekend." Ian's dad always said her name like Ian should care about who she was. As if she was important to him now. "The wedding is around the corner, and we're really behind with a lot of stuff."

"It's okay, I understand," Ian said.

"Weekend?" Davey said. He was still calm. He just wanted some reassurance that it was happening.

"You're busy. Maybe the next one?" Ian's tone was low. He was hoping Davey would get interested in something else.

"That's what I was gonna suggest," his dad said. The muffling sound returned. "Actually, it might have to be the one after that. I'm telling you, Ian, when it's your turn to get married, you should elope. It's a lot easier." His dad laughed.

Davey moved over to him.

"Weekend!" Davey shrieked. He knew what was happening. He may not have understood why his dad was no longer at home, but he understood when plans were changing. When his schedule was changing.

It always surprised adults when Davey put things like that together. But Ian was used to it. He was used to his brother being smarter than he was supposed to be.

"Daddy! Weekend!" Davey continued.

Ian's mom walked in the room.

"What's going on?" she asked.

Abruptly, Davey turned and ran toward her with his arms out. He was going for her throat. Melissa grabbed Davey's arms and held them above his head. Both Ian and Melissa had been trained on how to "prone contain" Davey. It was supposed to help them if Davey had meltdowns. It never did.

"Davey, no!" Ian's mom said sternly as she wrestled with her son.

"Is Davey all right?" his dad asked.

Ian wanted to tell him that Davey was bawling. That everything would be a lot easier if he was around.

"Dad, I gotta go. We'll call you about the weekend after next." Ian hung up the phone. He ran over and pulled Davey away from his mom. She was about five foot six and weighed 130 pounds. Davey was almost a half foot taller and weighed closer to 175.

Together they got Davey to the ground. Then they moved anything out of the way that he might try to kick or knock over.

Davey continued to cry, then he started to scream. Ian wondered how it must've sounded to the neighbors.

Davey was really upset and screamed for a long time.

Ian and his mom turned away from Davey. They could still see him through their peripheral vision, but it was best to act like they were ignoring the outburst. Ian could feel his mom's eyes on him, but he wouldn't look back.

It was at times like these that Ian hated his family. Worse than that, he hated himself for feeling this way. He wanted to be strong for his mom, and for the most part he was. Still, deep down he blamed her for driving his father away. It wasn't fair that Ian's father got to be free from all of this.

Ian didn't spend a lot of time dwelling on what was and wasn't fair. He knew it was a waste of energy.

CHAPTER 11

Me and Davey

The next afternoon Ian played with Davey after his first varsity practice. It had gone really well. Steve Morgan wasn't there, so Ian got to play his position right off. Everybody was really cool to him—with the exception of Andre Evans and Jeff Bruns, Steve's best friends. They may have been bigger guys, but Ian knew they were a little slower than the smaller junior varsity players.

The best part was getting to see Jessica cheer. Ian didn't make any great plays, but he played a lot, caught a bunch of passes, and held his own. Jessica, looking perfect as ever in her breezy white-and-black cheerleader practice outfit, got to see it all.

"This would validate her choosing me for sure," he thought. They made plans to hang out later that night. Ian really wanted to take advantage of the little bit of summer that was left before school started.

That afternoon, Ian and Davey were home alone. It was a rare time of calm, and Ian was in a reflective mood. As they played with Davey's toys, Ian did his best to be into it. The problem was that Davey would ask Ian to play, then wouldn't pay any attention. If Ian said no, then Davey might throw a tantrum.

Ian's mom and dad had bought Davey a bunch of toys. They tried to make them ones that a fourteen-year-old might play with. Car sets, a toy video camera, a Nintendo DS, but Davey didn't seem to care about them. He might look at the toy for a little bit, maybe even play with it a few times, but he'd always go back to his *Ice Age* dolls, Thomas the Tank Engine, or some random stuffed animal. About the only technology he showed any interest in was the iPad. Ian's mom couldn't afford one, but Davey could use his father's when they stayed at his house.

The older Ian got, the more he found himself watching his brother when they were together as opposed to interacting with him.

"You don't play with your toys," Ian wanted to say to his brother. "You just line them up, one right next to the other, and then when you get them just right in your mind, you put them away. That's not really playing with them."

When Ian was younger, he didn't notice how different his brother was. It didn't matter then. But the older they got, the more Ian couldn't ignore it.

It didn't bother him that Davey was different. It just bothered Ian that he had to live a different life than everybody else because of his brother.

CHAPTER 12

The News

Ian knew something was up when his mom took him to Jimmy's Burrito Factory for the second time that week. She never did that. Ian probably would have been more on his game, but he and Jessica had been up late the night before on the phone. They hadn't really talked about anything important, but Ian found himself so excited to be talking with her that he just kept the conversation going.

One day he was going to tell her about Davey. And when he did, she wouldn't care because she would know the real Ian. She would be so in love with him none of that would matter. They would just have to get there first.

Melissa was staring at Ian more than usual as she spoke, "You two have never been in school together because they didn't have an autism-specific class. The school district recently decided to add one."

As Melissa talked, Ian found it really hard to concentrate. What was she talking about?

"So where will Davey's new class be?" Ian finally asked. He figured maybe Davey would be going to school far away. Maybe his mom wouldn't be able to be around as much because she would be driving Davey back and forth. Ian would actually have some time to himself. Have Jessica come over ...

"It's going to be at Davis High School. Davey's going to be at the same school as you now."

Melissa stared at Ian after she said that. She was trying to gauge if this was sinking in with him.

"What!" Ian couldn't believe what he'd just heard.

"I knew this was gonna be hard for you. That's why I wanted us to have the afternoon to ourselves so we could talk about it." Ian's mom touched his hand.

"But ... we've never been in school together." Ian pulled his hand away.

"I'm sorry, honey."

"What if I go back to Hawks? Can't I do that? I didn't get in trouble there or anything. I only left because we moved. I didn't even really get started there."

"You can't. You have to go to your home school and that's Davis. It won't be so bad. Everybody loves Davey once they get to know him."

How many times had Davey had problems in school? How many times had Ian been happy that he had been nowhere in sight when the bad reports came home? Like the time Davey bit a kid on the playground. Or when he destroyed school property. And the meltdowns ... so many meltdowns.

Now Davey was going to be at Davis High School.

Everybody would see him when he had problems. When he acted out and screamed and cried. And even if he didn't have problems, he looked different. His nose ran, and he wiped it on his shirt. He'd pick his nose and eat it. It was a major effort for him to do the simplest things. For him to say the simplest things.

"Everybody will see this now," Ian thought to himself. Everybody will know. This was like a nightmare coming true.

School had always been Ian's sanctuary. No matter what happened at home—with Davey or his mom and dad—he could be somebody else at school. Somebody who didn't have problems at home. He didn't have disconnected parents and he didn't have an autistic brother.

That was all over now.

Off Practice

Ian sat on the bench watching the varsity team practice. The heat was awful, but Ian hardly noticed. He was still reeling from the news that Davey was going to be in school with him.

Making matters worse was the fact that Steve Morgan was at practice. Nobody talked about why he randomly had to miss certain days.

"He's a senior and probably doing stuff to get ready for college," Ian told himself. "Steve's one of those people who has money. His parents' money. He's going places. The world is wide open for people like him. They never have any problems."

With Steve at practice, it seemed like even more players, not just Andre and Jeff, were showing Ian that he wasn't welcome on the team. He'd say hi but be ignored. When Ian did get to play, it seemed like the other players were going out of their way to take him down.

For added pressure, he wasn't playing well at all. He was so caught up in thinking about what everybody else was thinking that he wasn't trusting his own instincts.

As he watched Steve play, he saw how effortless it was for him. He just glided past all those guys who were bigger and stronger.

"Will I ever look like that on varsity?" Ian wondered. "Maybe I left junior varsity too soon. At least there I was somebody.

Here? I'm not needed unless Steve isn't around. I'm a human afterthought."

Ian had a feeling Steve was going to go out of his way to be at practices and games now. There was no way he was going to give Ian any of his glory. He didn't ask anybody why Steve wasn't able to always be there, but he figured they wouldn't tell him anyway.

Ian's one saving grace was that the varsity cheerleaders weren't practicing today. "If Jessica was here, she probably wouldn't even talk to me." He was in full pity mode now.

Eventually, Ian's second varsity practice was over. As he walked with the other players to the locker room, he realized that this wasn't how it was supposed to be. It was the day before his first year officially playing varsity and he was miserable.

CHAPTER 14

First Day Back

Ian squinted at the sun as he approached Davis High School. He hadn't gotten much sleep the night before. Having anxiety about being in school with his brother was a new feeling. Ian had heard his mom getting Davey ready that morning, and Ian wanted to be out of the house well before the bus came to pick Davey up. He always wondered what the neighbors really thought when the small yellow bus stopped in front of their house.

A bunch of students were out in the front of the school. Some were going over their schedules, others were texting or talking on their phones, and others were just chilling out against the wall or sitting on the curb. The school was open, and Ian saw more students inside.

"I just need to stick to my plan," he told himself. It was simple: he was going to avoid Davey.

If he did it correctly, he could make it so they never saw each other. Ian had seen Davey's schedule, and he realized that with the exception of PE, Davey never left room 415. Davey had PE second period. Ian, since he was an athlete, had it sixth because it went right into football practice. And Ian's classes were nowhere near room 415.

During snack and lunch, most of the kids with special needs ate in the cafeteria. When they were done, they basically stayed there. They only left when they were having a problem or getting upset. If that happened, then they went back to their classroom to calm down.

"The food in the cafeteria sucks. I have no reason to go in there anyway," Ian reasoned. He always brought his lunch.

Now there was always the possibility that Ian might run into Davey in the halls. "If I keep my guard up and hang out in the areas of school where I know Davey will never be—like the English, math, and science buildings—I'll be okay." Ian also had another advantage: Davey's schedule, the one that was written on the whiteboard at home and at school.

Melissa always wrote out Davey's daily schedule. Since not knowing the schedule gave Davey a lot of anxiety, his mom would repeat it to him several times. As long as Ian knew that schedule, he would know what his brother was going to be doing before, during, and after school.

Ian took a deep breath as he walked through the large gate leading into the school. As he made his way to his locker, he said hi to some friends and football players. He knew that any minute now Davey would be arriving on the bus.

Ian double-checked his combination. Then he took out his class list and looked at it:

First Period—Algebra 2
Second Period—English
Third Period—Biology

As Ian made his way over to the math building, he made mental notes of where all his classes were. He tried to figure out ways he could get to each class without being seen. Ian figured he had a pretty good routine too.

"Davey's not the only one with a hyper-organized schedule now," Ian said under his breath.

On Display

You're gonna have to help me in my math class, Ian. Mrs. Gerlich seems so mean," Jessica said with a smile.

"No problem," Ian said.

Jessica had the same math teacher as Ian during a different period. They were comparing their schedules even though Ian had memorized hers when she showed it to him a few days before.

Ian and Jessica were talking in the school plaza, which was right next to the cafeteria. All of the classes had let out early because there was going to be a "Welcome Back" performance there. The plaza was one of the places Ian avoided because it was so open. The only problem was that Jessica was in the performance. She had asked Ian to be there. She said it would make her feel good to know he was watching her.

"I can't wait until this year is over. Then I don't have to take math again until college," Jessica stated.

"I'll probably need your help in English," Ian offered. "I'm awful at that."

"I've never gotten math," Jessica continued.

"And I've never gotten English." Ian smiled.

"That's why we're perfect together. We balance out." She took his hand in hers. Ian looked her in the eye. They kissed slowly. Ian almost couldn't believe it was happening. He'd never kissed a girl at school. For those brief moments when their lips touched, Ian was able to forget about everything. Everything he was hiding.

"Come on, Jess!" Amanda called to her. Jessica turned and looked at her. She wasn't blushing, but Ian felt like he was. "Stop kissing your boyfriend. Let's get on stage."

"Your boyfriend." Amanda had called Ian Jessica's *boyfriend*. The best part? Jessica didn't say he wasn't. That meant Ian had a chance with her.

She smiled at Ian. Then Jessica laughed as she ran over to Amanda. They had a quick exchange between them, then more laughter as they headed for the stage. Ian had noticed that girls seemed to laugh together without saying anything. He'd like to be able to do that with someone.

The school band assembled on stage and started playing. Drums sounded, horns blared, and out came the cheerleaders doing their routines. Jessica wasn't in the center of it all, but as far as Ian was concerned, she may as well have been.

There was something about Jessica's smile. It didn't seem forced. She really loved being on stage, moving to the music, and cheering for the school. She wasn't fake. She may have been popular and sought after by other guys, but she didn't seem to care about that. She was a real person, and that's why Ian liked her.

Amidst all this, Ian noticed Davey and Greg walking with the other students in Davey's class. As they made their way over to the cafeteria, Ian watched his brother. When Davey wasn't watching TV or playing with his toys, his eyes always looked angry, like he was being forced to do something unpleasant. Since he didn't exercise much, he weighed more than most kids his age. Walking with his mouth hung open, there was no way that anybody looking at him wouldn't know he had special needs.

"Come on, Davey!" Ian wanted to yell. "Get your act together." But he didn't. Ian couldn't. Deep down he knew none of this was really Davey's fault. It was nobody's fault. It was just the way things were.

Davey and most of the other kids in the class moved past the music without paying any attention to it. If it had been Disney music or *Blues Clues*, Ian was certain that Greg wouldn't be able to pull Davey away.

Right before Ian went back to watching Jessica, he made eye contact with Greg. It was brief, but it was long enough for Ian to know he had slipped up. It was only the first day and Ian had gotten too comfortable.

He started to turn away but Greg smiled and waved. It all happened so quickly. The only thing Ian could think to do was look away. Then he discreetly moved behind some people and made his way out of the plaza.

Ian had been quick but not quick enough to miss the look of surprise and disappointment on Greg's face.

Big Leagues

Davis High School was playing Jones High School. The stands on both sides of the Davis field were packed with students and parents. From Ian's perspective it sounded like everybody was cheering.

When he looked over at the Jones players, he realized just how out of his league he might be. Like the varsity players on the Davis team, these guys were massive.

Ian thought, "If these guys tackle me at full speed … I'm dead."

And that was a distinct possibility on this night since Steve was out. It had been a last-minute thing. Nobody talked about it. Coach Banks just informed the team that Ian was going to be subbing for him. This news was met with little enthusiasm from the rest of the team.

Standing on the field right as the first game of the season was underway, Ian Taylor had an unsettling thought: "I shoulda stayed on junior varsity." As quickly as that thought appeared in his head, he blocked it out. Ian had a job to do.

With only thirty seconds left on the clock, the score was Davis 14, Jones 15. Davis had just gained possession of the ball, and they were poised to run a game-winning play at the twenty-yard line.

"Okay," Carlos Ortega, the quarterback for Davis, ordered, "We're gonna press this all the way."

Then he looked at Ian. Ian had been ignored almost the whole game. There were plenty of opportunities for Carlos to pass the ball to him, but he never took them. Either he didn't think Ian could do it, or he wasn't going to give Ian the satisfaction of making a play in a game Steve should have been playing.

"Ian, I'm probably gonna throw it to you, so get behind the line."

"Okay," Ian said.

He was going to show Carlos and the rest of the team that he deserved to be there.

All the players got in their positions. Ian stared at where Carlos told him to be. He could feel himself breathing heavier and heavier. This was it.

The play was run.

Ian used all the speed he had and ran behind the line. Since he had been ignored the entire game, the Jones players really weren't paying attention to him.

"Maybe that was the plan all along," Ian guessed.

Then he had another thought. "Is Davey here?"

If he was, how would Ian avoid him after the game? Would he ditch his family and call them on his cell phone? Make up an excuse for why he had to see them later? He glanced over at the stands to see if he could see his mom and Davey.

And then in an instant Ian saw the ball in the air. It was coming toward him. Ian brought up his hands, but it wasn't right. He wasn't right. He wasn't thinking.

And the ball went through his hands and smacked into his chest. As Ian tried to wrap his arms around it, the ball fell to the grass.

In his first varsity game, Ian Taylor had fumbled the ball.

After the Game

Ian walked over to his mom and Todd after the game. As nobody was congratulating him, talking to him, or even looking at him, Ian had no problem getting over to them. They were waiting on the field. Davey wasn't there, so Ian felt okay going over.

Melissa wore a look on her face like she knew Ian was bummed about what happened. Todd stared at Ian like he didn't know what to say. Ian thought Todd was all right. He wore jeans and T-shirts and wasn't some stuffy guy. However, Ian knew he was too into his mom. His mom liked Todd, but she didn't seem crazy about him. He was too nice. For some reason Melissa didn't seem to want guys who genuinely liked her. Who were good for her. It was like she had a defense mechanism up that would keep her from getting close to anybody but her kids.

Also, most of the guys barely looked at Ian and Davey. Ian figured two kids were a lot of baggage. But two kids and one with autism? *That* was a deal breaker.

"You played great," Melissa said, giving Ian a hug.

"Good game, Ian," Todd started. "It's pretty impressive that you're on varsity as a sophomore."

"Not after the way I played tonight," Ian said dejectedly.

"Davey was gonna come, but he changed his mind at the last minute. I got Mr. and Mrs. Tullai to stay with him," his mom said.

"That should make their night fun," Ian mumbled. What Ian didn't say was that it was his fear of Davey being there that had made him lose his concentration.

Davey had made him lose the game, and he wasn't even there.

That was a good thing, Ian reminded himself. How would he have gotten away from his mom if Davey was there? She always waited for Ian on the field. *If* Davey didn't make her leave before the game was over, that is.

"Well, I'm gonna go shower. I'll see you at home. Thanks for coming. Sorry I sucked." Ian walked away.

"You want a ride home?" Ian's mom was startled by his abruptness.

"Nah, I'll walk. Go out. Have a good time." He just wanted to be alone.

On his way to locker room, Ian started to think about where he was going to go after he showered and changed. The

Tullais were with Davey so that meant Ian's night was free. Maybe he'd just go on a long walk.

"Ian," Jessica ran over to him. "I saw you talking to your mom. I wanted to meet her."

Ian turned and saw Melissa and Todd entering the parking lot.

"I'm sorry. They're gone now." Ian wanted to sound cheerful. To not call any more attention to his fumble, especially in front of Jessica, but he couldn't. "I guess I blew that game."

"No way," Jessica asserted.

"You're being nice. I fumbled the ball."

"Carlos could've thrown it to you a million times before that. Why did he wait until the end of the game?" Jessica wasn't lying. She didn't think it was Ian's fault.

"Well, nobody's gonna be talking about that," Ian grumbled. "They're gonna be talking about how the sophomore blew the game."

"No, they won't," Jessica countered. "They'll forget all about it when you make a big play in the next one."

"I might not play. It depends on if Steve's here or not."

Ian realized it was the first time he had ever brought up Steve Morgan in front of Jessica. She never talked to Ian about him. He never asked. It seemed better that way.

"You'll play. Even if he is here next week. You'll play in a lot more games."

"Thanks," Ian said. He had been really bummed about the game, but somehow Jessica wiped all that away.

"Jordana's having a party. You wanna go?" Jessica beamed as she changed the subject.

Jordana was another cheerleader. Ian didn't really know her.

Ian really wanted to be alone with Jessica. He wanted to go on one of their walks. He wanted to kiss her and forget all about the game and the rest of his life.

Jessica was a cheerleader, though. She was popular. She would want to go to the party, and Ian didn't want to hold her back.

"Sure. If you don't mind being seen with the Davis High School fumbler."

"I'm honored to be seen with you," Jessica said, flashing the smile that had just about knocked Ian over when he first saw her on the field.

They started to kiss. It was long and slow. Jessica always smelled so good. She always felt so good. He hoped she thought the same about him.

Party

Jessica drove them to the party. They chit-chatted during the drive. Ian didn't know what he wanted or what he was supposed to get from these conversations. He always found himself trying to impress Jessica. That's why losing the game for the team was so hard for him.

"How can I impress her now?" he couldn't help but wonder.

Had they won, things would've been different. Now he found himself struggling for things to say.

He was relieved when they got to Jordana's house.

The party was a mix of everybody who went to Davis. There were football players, cheerleaders, basketball players, baseball players, people in clubs, brainiacs, nerds … it was only at parties that all these worlds collided.

Ian was standing near Jessica in the kitchen. They were talking with Amanda and Kaitlyn Cohen. Ian had talked with Shawn and Ryan a little when he arrived. They couldn't believe he was actually hanging out. Ian hadn't realized it, but he couldn't remember the last time he'd just hung with friends on a Friday night.

As Jessica, Amanda, and Kaitlyn talked, Ian noticed that Andre and Jeff were standing next to them. Steve's best friends. They had acknowledged Ian with a what's-up? head nod when they first saw him, but beyond that there had been no other communication between them. But Ian wondered if they'd be talking to him now even if he *had* made the game-winning touchdown.

"You guys will never like me as long as you see me as somebody trying to muscle out Steve," Ian wanted to say.

Somehow all the conversations got mingled together. Everybody in the kitchen was talking to one another.

"Dude, no way," Andre started. "Your ass was so scared when Mrs. Simone called you out for eating."

Jessica, her friends, and some others standing around laughed.

"This guy," Jeff continued—it was apparent he had shared this story with others before—"I'm sitting there enjoying my morning maple bar and he starts trying to steal a piece. When I refused to give him one, he got all butt hurt, so he told Mrs. Simone I was eating."

Everybody cracked up. Ian laughed but he wasn't really laughing. He didn't like these guys, but it was because they didn't like him.

"They made him go sit outside next to the retard class." Andre laughed.

Everybody else did as well.

Ian felt himself grow cold all over. The retard class. That was room 415. Davey's class. There were other special day classes on the campus, but 415 was the one with the kids who looked and acted the least normal. They had to be talking about it.

"Is it me or do we have a lot more of them in our school this year?" someone asked. Ian figured the guy didn't have anything against the special day class. He was just trying to be in on the conversation. In with Jeff and Andre.

"I saw all of them walking through the campus. I was like, 'What is up with that?' " Jeff commented.

He started to imitate the way one of them walked. Ian grew even colder when he realized the person Jeff was imitating was Davey. His eyes were wide, his walk was labored, and his mouth hung open. Who else could it be?

Everybody was laughing. They were laughing at the retards. Ian smiled nervously. He looked over at Jessica. She was laughing as well. Ian's smile vanished.

"So much for Jessica being a real person," Ian thought.

He wanted to get mad. He wanted to yell at Jessica. He wanted to grab Jeff and Andre and tell them that nobody made fun of his brother.

Ian Taylor wanted to do a lot of things, but he was at a party and he was supposed to be having a good time. So he did nothing.

Confrontation with Greg

School had been in session for a little over two weeks. So far Ian's plan of avoiding Davey had been working great. In fact, much to Ian's surprise, Davey hadn't had any public meltdowns (that he saw, anyway). Coach Banks was working them so hard in varsity practice after school that Ian was also avoiding Greg at Davey's ABA sessions at home. Things had been going so well that Ian actually felt normal. Too normal.

He was walking back to biology class from the bathroom when Greg spotted him. Ian figured Greg must be on his break. At first Ian thought about dodging Greg. Greg would be shocked, but Ian didn't care. As he had done before, Ian thought about it for too long and it gave Greg time to wave and walk over. Ian wasn't going anywhere.

"What's up, Ian?" Greg asked. Ian couldn't tell if Greg was trying to mess with him. He knew that Greg knew what he'd been doing. "Am I gonna see my favorite varsity player get to play next game or not?"

"I don't know," Ian said. He couldn't think of anything else to say. He was too busy worrying if anybody else was going to see him talking to Greg. To see that he was buddies with the person who helped the retards. "I gotta get back to class."

Ian started to move past Greg. Greg positioned himself slightly in front of Ian.

Greg was glaring at Ian now. Ian half thought Greg was going to take him down, like he'd seen him take Davey down. Ian wasn't small but Greg was twice his size. "You're being a jerk, Ian."

Then, to make matters worse, Ian saw Peter Carreon and Jason McAlister, two guys on the varsity team who he didn't really know, walking across the hallway about a hundred feet from them. If these guys saw Ian, he was a dead man.

"I'm not doing anything." Ian side-stepped Greg and continued walking to class.

"It's not cool, Ian. Your mom would be bummed," Greg stated as Ian felt his eyes burn into his back.

Ian didn't care if Greg was mad at him. Right then, he didn't even care if Greg told his mom how he was avoiding Davey. The only thing Ian cared about was if Peter and Jason had seen him talking to Greg. But in fact, it didn't seem like they had seen Ian at all.

CHAPTER 20
Practice

Ian was feeling pretty good about practice. Steve had been there for half of it, then he had to leave. Nobody said why or made any comments, which was weird. But this gave Ian a chance to play, so he didn't care. Coach Banks was having them do a scrimmage, and the side Ian was now playing on was moving down the field.

Another play was run and Ian found himself wide open. Miguel, the quarterback for Ian's side, saw Ian and threw him the ball. This was going to be easy. He was back in his zone. Practice was going to be over soon and he felt great.

"I could play another scrimmage after this," he told himself.

The ball was practically in his hands when Ian was blindsided by Andre. The second Ian felt Andre's massive frame against his, he knew it was on purpose. Andre slammed into him, body checking the smaller Ian to the ground.

It hurt. Big time. He felt like he had been hit by a car.

Ian lay on the ground, trying to come to his senses. He knew he had to get up quickly because if he didn't, Andre would know he'd hurt him. Ian sat up slowly, remembering he had heard somewhere that if you got up too quickly, you could hurt yourself even worse. All the players gathered around him.

Ian got to his feet. He felt sick. His body ached and his head was throbbing.

"Sorry," Andre said. He didn't even look at Ian as he walked away.

"No, you're not," Ian said. He was furious. He felt himself losing control. Ian was so used to keeping his feelings bottled up inside. "You did that on purpose! You did it for Steve. Well, he's not here and I am, so you better get used to it."

Andre turned and looked at Ian. "You won't be here for long." Andre laughed. "Coach is gonna see you can't hang with us, JV boy."

Jeff walked over and stood by Andre. Nobody on the team knew what to do. They just watched what was going on. Andre moved close to Ian.

"You blew the last game! You're nothing but a skinny punk pretending he can play here."

Ian knew he should just let this go. But he couldn't. He was getting even madder. Suddenly he couldn't feel any of the pain from Andre's cheap shot.

"And you're just a fat, slow senior

who isn't gonna be anything when he tries to play in college." Ian was digging his own grave, but he didn't care. He'd been treated like crap by these guys for long enough.

Andre moved even closer.

"And you're retarded," he said slowly. His tone was low so only Ian could hear him. "Like your brother," he hissed.

In an instant Ian grabbed Andre by his helmet guard. He pulled him down and kicked and punched him as hard as he could. With all the padding Andre was wearing, Ian doubted his blows were hurting him. Still, Ian was quick and he had the upper hand, so he kept going.

Andre crouched down. He lifted Ian up, then slammed him to the ground. Ian knew this was going to compound his injuries. Andre sat on top of Ian and rained down punches. Ian covered up, expecting to be annihilated, but it never happened.

"Get the hell off him, Andre!" Coach Banks shrieked as he pulled him off Ian. "You guys are a team. Save it for Cliffmore on Friday."

"He started it, Coach!" Andre yelled.

"Don't give me that," Coach Banks barked back. He was furious.

Ian just lay on the grass. He wondered if he could get up again.

"You've been riding Taylor since he got on the team. He deserves to play varsity. Leave him alone. Let's finish this scrimmage!"

All the players started to get in their formations.

"Not you, Andre! You're running fifteen laps," Coach Banks bellowed.

"What about him?" Andre pointed to Ian.

"He's doing five. Now help him up, and let's stay focused on what we have to do out here!" Coach Banks stormed off.

To Ian's surprise, some of the varsity players actually helped him get to his feet.

Ian limped over to the track and began to run five laps. Andre had already gotten started; he was halfway done with his first one.

Ian didn't care. The only thing on his mind was Andre's comment about him being a retard like Davey. Ian was mad about that comment, but he was also angry at something else. For all of his work, for all the distance he tried to place between himself and his brother, Andre had still found out about him.

"Eventually everybody will know," Ian reasoned. The best thing he could do was to continue doing what he was doing. He wasn't in any hurry to be truthful.

CHAPTER 21

Talk with Mom

Ian and his mom sat at the kitchen table finishing their dinner. She served grilled chicken and rice. She sipped a glass of wine while Ian was trying to decide if he wanted seconds.

"So tell me," Melissa started, "how's school? What's it like having Davey in your world?"

"It's awful," Ian wanted to say, but he didn't.

Davey could be heard in the next room laughing and talking as he watched *The Iron Giant* for the millionth time. He had seen that movie so many times he could recite every word. And he did.

"It's okay. We don't really see each other," Ian stated. He figured he wasn't really lying. He just wasn't saying he avoided his brother.

"What about your classes?"

"They're good." Ian wasn't lying about that. So far he hadn't missed any assignments and hadn't gotten any grade lower than a B on any of his tests.

Melissa stared at him. She could tell by his answers that he wasn't being honest with her.

"I know this is tough for you, Ian." His mom's voice was serious. She wasn't trying to make it seem as if Ian needed to like his situation. He just had to accept it. "But you'll have your own life someday. Like when you go off to college."

"That's three years away," Ian blurted

out. He couldn't help himself. Would he really be able to dodge having to deal with Davey for three whole years? If Andre knew about Davey, everybody would know.

Jessica would know—eventually.

"Three years isn't *that* long."

"Who's gonna pay for it? We had to move because the other house cost too much."

Melissa stared at Ian, then nodded her head.

"That isn't something you need to worry about. Your father will be involved too. You're gonna go off to college and play football. The only reason you won't is if you don't want to." Melissa stared Ian dead in the eyes.

"You think Dad will help me?" Ian asked.

"He better." She smiled. "No, he will. He loves you."

Ian heard that a lot. From his mom, his dad, his grandparents.

"He loves you," people would say to him.

But did he really? Ian figured that once his dad got free, he would start a new family and forget all about him and Davey.

"And I love you," Melissa went on. "That's why I want to know how you're handling Davey being in school with you."

Ian wanted to be honest. He wanted to tell his mom it was hell. That he avoided his brother like the plague. That he pretended he didn't know Davey, Greg, or anybody having anything to do with the special day class. That he wished his brother would just go away so Ian could enjoy school again. His refuge.

He decided he was going to do it. Ian was going to be honest with his mom about Davey.

"Well," he started.

Melissa's cell phone rang. She looked to see who it was. Todd's name flashed across the screen.

"I gotta take this. Todd said he needed to talk to me tonight." Melissa picked up the phone and walked into the kitchen.

"What about me?" Ian wondered to himself. "I need you too." He sat there staring at his food. He wasn't hungry anymore.

"Okay ..." Melissa's nervous tone in the next room broke into his thoughts. "I just ... I thought we'd worked that out. ... I've tried, Todd. ... What do you want from me?"

Ian had heard his mom have this conversation a bunch of times before. She dated a guy until he wanted to get serious. Then she pushed him away so he'd break up with her. So she wouldn't have to get close to him.

Ian's mom continued to talk with Todd as he got up from the table and walked down the hall to his room.

He passed Davey, who was too involved in his movie to notice him.

Ian wasn't too mad at his mom for taking Todd's call instead of talking to him. He knew what it felt like to want to have a life of your own. To want a life away from the people you called your family.

CHAPTER 22

Scoreboard

Davis was down by three points against Lianna High School. The game had been close, but Davis made some mistakes that allowed Lianna to take advantage.

Ian watched this home game from the bench feeling frustrated. He wasn't saying anything, though. Now he understood that if he was going to play on varsity—with basically the entire team not liking him—the only thing he was going to worry about was what he did on the field. As far as he was concerned, these bigger and more experienced guys were not necessarily better at the sport of football than he was.

The proof was in the next play. Steve got sacked because he wasn't being properly defended. He lay clutching his leg as the school medics came over and attended to him. Everyone in the stadium cheered when Steve finally got up. The medics helped him off the field.

"Taylor, get in there!" Coach Banks yelled.

Ian stood up, put on his helmet, and walked by Steve as he made his way onto the field.

"You okay?" Ian asked. He was always nice to people who weren't nice to him. Having a brother like Davey just made him more sensitive to other people's feelings.

Steve just nodded his head as the medics sat him down on the bench.

Ian felt like a million eyes were on him as he ran across the field and joined his team. He looked at the scoreboard and saw that there was less than a minute left.

Davis was at the twenty-yard line. There was a slim chance that they could outmaneuver Lianna and score a touchdown. Lianna was playing strong defense.

"Just go long, Taylor," was all Carlos said.

"Wait a minute," Ian wondered, "they're pinning what might be the final play on me again?" Aloud, Ian said, "Okay." He looked out at the stands and saw his mom. With Davey.

Davey wasn't really watching the game. Mom had brought their portable DVD player. Davey was no doubt watching one of the movies he always watched. Thankfully, he wasn't laughing loudly, slapping his legs, or hanging all over his mom like he did when a movie got him over stimulated. He almost looked normal.

Before Ian knew what was happening, the play was run. He moved past all the players from Lianna, and as he turned a few yards from the goal line, the ball was soaring. Effortlessly, Ian moved forward, jumped into the air, and felt the football land perfectly in his hands. For some reason it felt heavier, harder. Then, at the same time, Ian landed on the ground and made the touchdown.

The Davis side cheered. The game was over.

Ian had done it. He had scored the game-winning touchdown.

Ian felt victorious.

All the Davis players rushed him. In no time, he was up on two players' shoulders. As he was paraded around the field, he noticed both Andre and Jeff cheering for him.

Ian was high-fiving people he didn't even know. People who had never spoken to him before were yelling his name. But what mattered more was that Ian had finally shown everybody that Coach Banks was right. He belonged on varsity.

Ian Taylor was a hero.

When Ian was finally put down on the ground, he quickly went back into avoid-Davey mode. Ian saw his mom putting the portable DVD player away, then she helped Davey down the bleachers. They were no doubt headed for the field. Ian had one ace up his sleeve: they hadn't seen him yet.

People were still coming up to congratulate him. Ian wanted to soak it all in. He wanted to hug his mom and give Davey a high five. Davey probably hadn't seen Ian make the game-winning play, but his mom would surely tell him.

As the crowd on the field started to thin out, Ian made a beeline for the locker room. His phone was there. He was going to text his mom. He'd tell her that he saw them at the game. He'd say he got swept away by the team and that he'd see them later. Davey wouldn't want to wait, so they wouldn't stick around.

For Ian, it had been a successful night. He'd scored the game-winning touchdown and managed to avoid his family.

CHAPTER 23

Major Meltdown #1

All the good will from the game spilled over to Monday. Ian was treated like a celebrity. People came up to him to shake his hand, pat him on the back, and give him high fives. Even Steve, Andre, and Jeff were being cool. They actually talked to Ian about the upcoming game. Steve was going to play, but they thought maybe they could both get some time on the field.

"I need to stay on guard," Ian told himself. "How many people know my secret? Now that I made *the* play, will more people be curious about me?"

He certainly wasn't going to say anything.

Ian knew he couldn't pretend forever. He figured that if he continued to perform on the field, he would only get more popular. Eventually, he might become so cool that nobody, not even Steve, Andre, Jeff, or Jessica would care about Davey.

Ian found himself near the cafeteria at lunch. He tried to move past it as quickly as possible, but it was as if a supernatural power was leading him there at that precise time.

As he walked through crowds of students, he heard a shriek that was all too familiar to him.

"That's Davey," Ian told himself. He felt drawn to the cafeteria and took a peek inside.

Davey, who was eating with his class, raised his hand in the air, then brought it down on the face of one of the other special needs students. The student hardly seemed fazed and continued to eat his lunch. Davey then proceeded to wrap his hands around the student's throat.

As all of this was going on, the normal eating, talking, and texting continued. Nobody expected a public brawl. Ian had learned long ago that the rules of the world didn't apply to Davey Taylor.

As Greg ran over and pulled Davey away from the student he was attacking, Davey screamed, cried, and went after Greg. Davey threw awkward punches at Greg, who blocked the blows and talked to Davey in soothing tones. When Davey didn't stop, Greg grabbed Davey's arms and took him down. Greg was a big guy, and he made it look a lot easier than it was.

At this point, Davey entered full tantrum mode, with shrieks and cries. He used every bit of strength he had to fight off Greg. *Everybody* in the cafeteria was watching now.

"Davey!" Ian wanted to scream. "Stop it! You're melting down in front of the entire school!"

Ian found himself moving toward them involuntarily. He knew in situations like this that there was very little Greg could do to get Davey to calm down—Greg was now the source of Davey's anger. If Davey saw Ian—a familiar face not associated with the other events—that might help reduce his anxiety.

He was a few steps into the cafeteria when the bell rang. People started to leave, but nobody took their eyes off of Davey. Davey's class had finished eating and didn't seem to care about what was happening before their eyes.

Ian slowly turned and walked out of the cafeteria. "I have to get to class … this isn't my problem." At Davis High School, this was something he had to remember.

CHAPTER 24
Called Out

Ian put what happened with Davey and Greg out of his mind. He was settling into his computer science class. Mr. Wiseman sat at his desk doing the lesson on an ELMO projector. At first Ian wasn't able to concentrate, but the longer the class went, the more comfortable he became.

Then an aide walked in.

"Yes?" Mr. Wiseman looked up from his desk.

The aide walked over to him and spoke so none of the other students could hear her. Mr. Wiseman looked over at Ian. It was *the* look. He recognized the look. He knew what it meant: they needed help with Davey.

"Mr. Taylor, could you please go with the aide?" Mr. Wiseman's tone had a sense of urgency about it. Ian felt all the eyes in the classroom on him as he walked out with the aide.

Ian took a deep breath and walked into the cafeteria. Mr. Porter, the principal, eyed Ian as he walked over to them. The aide went back to the office.

Davey and Greg were on the ground, leaning up against the wall. As mad as Davey had been at Greg, he was now leaning against him. He held Greg like he held his mom after a tantrum. Davey had calmed down, but he was still crying. His eyes were filled with tears. Davey's face was red and puffy. He was breathing so fast that he was almost hyperventilating. Ian knew that Davey only got like this when he was really upset.

"We thought maybe if he saw you, he might calm down," Mr. Porter said.

"Okay," Ian said.

"You got this now?" he asked Greg.

"Yeah," Greg replied. He scratched Davey's back and squeezed his shoulders and arms. Davey liked all of those things, but it wasn't clear how much they were helping.

"Okay, let me know if you need anything." Mr. Porter walked away and started talking on his walkie talkie.

"I didn't tell them to call you. It was the principal's idea," Greg said. He glared at Ian. Ian knew that Greg had a lot of things he wanted to say to him.

A group of students walked through the cafeteria. They eyed Davey, Ian, and Greg. Ian knew if people at Davis hadn't put together that he and Davey were brothers yet, this event would certainly speed the process along.

127

"You feeling okay, Davey? Wanna go back to class?" Greg asked.

"No class," Davey said. His voice sounded like he was about to start crying again.

More students continued to move through the cafeteria. Some of them were members of the varsity team. They eyed Ian standing beside Davey and Greg. They gave him a what's-up? nod.

Ian thought any good feelings from his heroic touchdown were vanishing. Fast.

Then the cafeteria was empty again.

"How you feeling, Davey?" Ian asked.

Davey didn't look at him. He didn't respond at all. He just continued to breathe heavily and stare blankly at the wall.

"We'll go back to class soon. Right, Davey?" Greg said. He gave him a big squeeze.

"Class soon," Davey said. He continued to stare vacantly at the wall.

"You can go back to class," Greg said. "We don't need you." His eyes burned through Ian.

Ian stood there for a little while longer. Then he turned and walked away.

CHAPTER 25

Weekend with Dad

Steve Morgan had decided to grace the football team with his presence the night before, so Ian hadn't had a chance to shine like he had done the previous Friday. Davis was playing Fry High School, the worst school in the district, and they beat them easily.

These were Ian's thoughts as he sat in front of the TV at his father's Los Angeles home. He was actually able to watch the movie *Project X* because Davey was busy with his dad's iPad. Davey loved the iPad. He mainly watched stuff on YouTube, but sometimes he opened Google Earth. He didn't really know what he was doing, he just liked the way the application took you to different places.

"I know why you always give him the iPad," Ian wanted to say to his dad. "It's because it keeps Davey quiet. And out of your hair. You don't have to do anything. Why do we even come here?"

Some weekends with their dad, it seemed like playing with the iPad was all Davey did. Melissa was always planning stuff for the boys. She wanted them to learn and experience new things. They'd go to the park, to museums, to movies, to the mall, out to eat … His dad would take away the iPad if Davey "got out of hand." Davey seemed to understand this, and that's what kept him in line most of the time.

To Ian this just wasn't fair.

"You get to have your own life away from your family. It's too easy for you." He knew he should stop thinking about this stuff. It just upset him too much.

Making all of this worse was the fact that his dad's fiancée, Amy, was also there. The two of them were running around the house, going back and forth about the plans for their wedding. Amy barely acknowledged the boys. She never talked to Davey. She seemed petrified of him. Ian didn't even know if they were going to be invited to the wedding.

And today he didn't care. He was just trying to enjoy relaxing on the couch, doing nothing. He'd probably get to his homework at some point. He thought about calling Jessica, but right now he just wanted to veg out. It wasn't always easy at their dad's house. Davey listened better to Melissa because she had him on a strict schedule. Dad never made any plans, so the chances of Davey having a meltdown were much greater.

As the movie played, Ian closed his eyes. Davey's laughter at a cartoon on YouTube rang in his ears. He could hear Dad and Amy discussing cakes and flowers for the wedding. Ian was happy to be out of town, but he knew he and his brother were better off at home.

CHAPTER 26

Big Game Benched

Ian's weekend blues were soothed at the prospect of playing Savage High School. This was a big game. Davis hadn't beaten Savage in ten years. They were the closest school to Davis, so they were naturally their biggest rival.

"You're gonna smoke those guys," someone said to Ian in the hallway.

"They haven't got anybody as fast as you," another person said.

Ian playing in the game was contingent

on Steve's absence. As luck would have it, Steve was out, so this gave Ian another opportunity to shine. To make his school proud. To make Jessica proud. It was another step up the cool ladder.

If he could do it …

The way people were talking, it sure sounded like they believed in him. Even if he washed out—which he was sure hoping wouldn't happen—it felt good no longer being in Steve Morgan's shadow.

The minute Ian was called into Coach Banks's office, he knew it was bad news. The only thing he didn't know was what the news was going to be.

Coach Banks was looking through some playbooks when Ian walked in.

"Have a seat." He smiled.

Ian figured if he was smiling, then he couldn't have screwed up that badly. With the playbooks out, maybe Coach Banks wanted to have a strategy session before practice. Maybe he was going to give Ian more responsibility.

"You won't be playing against Savage," Coach Banks said before Ian could even speak.

"Why?" Ian asked. He thought his whole reason for being on varsity was to cover Steve.

"Steve's gonna play this game. He didn't think he could. It turns out he can. So that's what's gonna happen. I'm telling you because I know you were probably looking forward to it."

"Yeah," Ian said. There went his chance to prove himself again. To cement his image at Davis as somebody cool. Even if his brother wasn't.

"Steve's been with me since he was a freshman. Between you and me, I think you'd give us a better chance to beat Savage, but the way I figure it, we've lost to them for ten years. Eleven sure isn't going to hurt any more." Coach Banks laughed after he said that. If he was trying to make Ian feel better, it was only marginally working. "But he's a senior, you're a sophomore. I figure we'll get 'em next year."

"Okay," Ian said. He wanted to argue. He didn't see why they both couldn't play. Ian didn't say anything else, though. Over the years he had realized that getting upset about things usually didn't change their outcome.

Coach Banks's phone rang. He answered it as Ian left his office.

After a fairly listless practice, Ian went back to the locker room. He had a missed call from Jessica on his cell phone. He wanted to talk to her. But he wasn't ready to tell her he wouldn't be playing in the biggest game of the season.

He'd been in someone else's shadow for practically his entire life. It wasn't fair. First Davey. Now Steve Morgan.

Explosion

Ian knew his mom was frazzled before her date because she wasn't talking to him or Davey. When she did talk, she gave Ian one word answers. No matter how busy she was, she always gave the boys some of her time. This wasn't the case tonight. She was already dressed and frantically moving around the kitchen. Ian didn't know who this new guy was, how she had met him, or any of the stuff she usually told him. He wanted to talk with her about not being able to play in the game against Savage. When he realized that wasn't going to happen, he went into his room and started his homework. He planned on talking with Jessica later that night and figured he could talk to her about missing the game. Davey would be busy with his toys or watching TV.

Suddenly Ian heard a scream, then he heard the sound of things falling in the living room.

"Davey," Ian said to himself.

He quickly got off his bed and ran into the living room. His mom was still in the kitchen making dinner. She was so preoccupied that she hadn't even noticed what had happened with Davey.

Some DVDs were on the ground as well as some knickknacks that the boys' mom had set up around the entertainment center. Davey stood, holding the DVD player. The TV was still working, but Davey was seconds away from ripping the unit out of the wall.

"DAVEY!" Ian yelled. Nobody ever yelled at Davey. That usually made his outbursts worse. "What happened?"

"No *Fairly Odd Parents*!" Davey yelled.

"It isn't on?" Ian asked. He was trying to calm Davey down.

"No!" Tears were forming in Davey's eyes. He had a whole system for how he watched TV. He was used to his shows being on at certain times. The TV schedule must have changed.

"What about On Demand?" Ian offered. He knew he could get *Fairly Odd Parents* playing that way.

"NO ON DEMAND! *FAIRLY ODD PARENTS* ON TIME!" Davey was so upset he could barely talk.

Ian picked up the controller. He brought up the On Demand screen. He was about to press the button for the show to come on.

Then Davey threw the DVD player at him. Ian managed to catch it and set it down.

"Davey, stop!" Ian shrieked.

Davey's eyes widened. Ian had scared him.

"Why are you both yelling?" Melissa called from the kitchen.

"Ahhhh!" Davey's hands went up and he went after Ian with everything he had.

Before Ian knew what was happening, he slugged Davey with a solid right hook.

Ian expected to feel bad.

But he didn't.

He felt good. And he wanted to do it again.

Ian was tired of sacrificing his life for his brother. He'd had enough of hiding at school. He was through with being picked on. Steve Morgan and the other guys could go to hell.

Ian Taylor was done with all of it.

Davey screamed louder because nobody had ever really fought back against him. He started to hit, kick, and bite Ian. Before either of them knew what was happening, Ian had thrown Davey to the ground and climbed on top of him.

Davey may have been big, but he was no match for Ian. Not in this state. In fact, Ian saw something in Davey's eyes that he hadn't ever seen before.

Fear.

He still tried to fight back, but Ian's punches were shorter and more accurate. He punched Davey in the face again. Davey's eyes got wide. He'd never been hit like this before. Ian continued hitting him. Davey's screams soon fell silent. Just as that happened, Ian felt Melissa pulling him off of his younger brother by his hair.

"IAN, STOP!" she yelled.

She pulled at his clothes and turned him so that he spun away from her.

Davey let out a blood-curdling shriek. It was so loud that Ian wouldn't have been surprised if the cops came to their house.

Davey wasn't fighting anymore. He was no longer mad about *Fairly Odd Parents* not being on. He was crying. His nose was bloody and his face was bruised from what Ian had done.

"Mommy!" Davey screamed. "I need your help!"

"Oh, Davey." Melissa went to the ground and scooped him into her arms. She kissed him. Then she glared at Ian. "Ian," Melissa hissed, "what *is* the matter with you?"

Ian was still filled with rage. He could hardly speak. As good as it had felt to unload on Davey, Ian knew Davey wasn't the problem. *Ian* was the problem. And his mother *and* father ... all of them. He knew it, but there was nothing he could do about it. This was his life. Ian knew he would go off again before leaving for college. He internalized too many emotions.

The doorbell rang. It was his mother's date.

Ian wondered what this new guy would think of the Taylor family. What would he think about Melissa consoling her teenage son on the floor? He wouldn't know what had happened. How Ian had been attacked by his brother. He wouldn't know how long this had been brewing. How long Ian had been living like a prisoner in his own life.

The doorbell rang again.

Ian walked back into his bedroom and shut the door.

Grounded

Melissa knocked so gently that Ian pretended he didn't hear it. He stared at his biology book, hoping she would just go away.

The knocking got louder, then Melissa walked into the room.

"Hey," she said.

"Hey," Ian offered back. He didn't look up from his book. "Where's your date?" Ian knew he was gone. He was pissed and didn't want his mom to forget it.

"He's gone." She gave a small chuckle. "Davey was in full meltdown." Ian's mom looked around his room. "It probably wouldn't have been that great of a night anyway."

Ian glanced up at his mom when she wasn't looking at him. She was still dressed like she was going out. He quickly looked back down at his book.

"Listen, Ian," Melissa started. "I know it isn't easy having a brother like Davey—"

"No, you don't!" Ian half yelled. He had gotten this same speech from his mom before, and he wasn't going to sit through it again. "You and Dad don't care. You do whatever you want with your lives, and you don't care what it does to me or Davey."

"Ian—"

"You. Don't. Care! Dad's getting married, and he's gonna have a whole new family. You'll meet a new guy next week, and you won't be around. You'll just leave me here to hang out with Davey. You don't care if I have a life. You don't care if he ruins school for me."

Melissa suddenly burst into tears.

Ian hadn't expected this, but he had to say something. He didn't mind his mom relying on him so much. He didn't mind that she expected him to act much older than he was. Ian just couldn't always handle being the responsible one. Not anymore.

"I'm sorry, Ian." Melissa collected herself quickly. The tears were still flowing but she was able to talk. "I'll try harder."

Ian just stared at his mom. He hadn't expected her to start crying. He couldn't imagine that his words had enough power to make an adult cry. Let alone somebody as tough and strong as his mom.

"Do you believe me?" she asked.

Ian nodded his head.

"Okay, now for the bad news." She was fairly composed now. There were almost no tears at all. "You're gonna have to be punished."

"Mom!" Ian was getting angry all over again. "This was the first time I ever hit him!"

"There have been other times." Melissa eyed him sharply.

Ian had forgotten, but there *had* been other times.

"But Davey always hits me. You …" Ian knew he shouldn't have hit his brother. He just lost control. Davey wasn't the smartest kid in the world, but didn't he at least know it was wrong to hit people?

"That's different," Melissa said.

"Why?"

"Because Davey isn't like you and me. You know he feels and thinks about things differently."

"Well, maybe I think about things differently," Ian offered up meekly. He knew he wasn't going to win this argument.

"Ian," Melissa glared at him. That look let him know this conversation was over. "You know it's wrong, and I don't need to explain it to you. I'm sorry about this, but it isn't going to be forever."

"It doesn't feel like you're sorry," he interjected.

"You're grounded for a week. Other than school and football practice, you're gonna be home."

"Oh, sure. So then you can go out with a bunch of guys whenever you want. Why isn't Davey being punished?"

"He'll be punished."

Melissa turned and walked out of Ian's room. He just sat there. He didn't want to do his homework. He didn't want to talk with Jessica. He just wanted to disappear.

A few minutes later, he heard his mom on the phone with whomever she'd canceled her date.

No Life

So you can't do anything after the game?" Jessica didn't sound mad, just surprised. They'd done something almost every Friday night since they'd started dating.

Ian realized that the more time they spent together, the more he liked her. He couldn't keep things casual forever. A girl like Jessica expected more. Deserved more. However, now was not the time to tell her the truth about his family.

"My mom freaked out over my biology progress report," he lied. "She says other than school and practice, I need to be at home studying for the next week."

"Oh ..." Jessica sounded happy to know this wouldn't last that long.

Ian hated lying to her. He knew it was only a matter of time before the way he was acting would come back to haunt him.

Something came over him. He stopped walking, pulled her toward him, and kissed her. It was slow and warm. Ian forgot about everything. He wanted some of what Jessica had to rub off on him.

"I really like you a lot, Jessica," he said softly. Ian hoped this would do the trick. Buy him some more time so he could figure everything out.

"I like you a lot too." Jessica's eyes were so inviting. So understanding. Ian kissed her again. He was starting to relax a little. "Maybe I can come over and help you study? I wanna meet your mom. You think she'll like me?"

"Yeah," Ian nodded his head. "But she specifically told me that part of my being grounded was no visitors."

They stared at each other and continued walking through the campus. It was a fairly mellow day. None of the clubs were doing anything at lunch. It was calm, just the way Ian liked it.

"Let's spend double the amount of time together next weekend, okay?" Jessica half asked, half stated.

"Yeah," Ian agreed. "Sounds good. That'd be awesome."

"It would be great if we could spend a whole day together." She smiled.

A whole day with Jessica. That's just what Ian needed. He felt normal when he was with her.

As Jessica continued to talk, Ian looked across the campus and saw Davey and Greg. Davey, a big smile on his face, walked in front of Greg. He moved through the campus quickly, laughing to himself. Ian figured Davey was probably thinking about something funny he'd seen or heard. Greg walked behind him, talking to another student.

Davey was in a good mood. If he saw Ian, he would surely come over to him.

And to Jessica.

"I've told my parents a lot about you," Jessica said. But Ian was already turning his body in the opposite direction.

"Hey, I need to see Coach Banks," Ian declared.

"Okay," Jessica said.

And then, in that one instant, Jessica saw Davey and Greg in the distance. Greg was looking at them. Davey hadn't seen Ian yet. When Jessica looked at Ian, he could tell she knew. She hadn't ever asked Ian about his brother. Maybe she didn't want to know the truth.

If there was ever a time for Ian to merge his worlds, this was it.

"I'll text you after practice," Ian said as he hastily moved toward the gym.

"Bye," Jessica said.

Ian couldn't get away fast enough.

Major Meltdown #2

Ian had been so bummed about being grounded—about not seeing Jessica, about everything—that he forgot to bring his lunch on Monday. He had money on him, but he didn't want to chance going into the cafeteria. Ian even considered the food kiosks, but they were too close to the cafeteria to risk it. He wanted to go off campus and buy lunch. But at Davis, you had to be at least a junior to do that. Jessica had gone off campus with her friends. Ian would've texted her, but he had also forgotten his phone. He just wasn't on it today.

He passed Steve and Andre by the drama room. They were eating pizza and drinking sodas.

"Hey, Ian," Steve called out.

Steve had been around more on the varsity team. He didn't seem so threatened by Ian any more. The other varsity players were being cooler to Ian too.

"Hey." Ian eyed their pizza. "Are they serving food like that in the cafeteria?"

"No." Andre laughed as he took a sip of his soda. "That stuff sucks. These are leftovers from a teacher party in the lounge."

"You want some? We were gonna go get more," Steve offered.

The teacher's lounge was behind the cafeteria. It was too close.

"Nah," Ian said.

"Come on," Steve said. He and Andre walked away, bringing Ian with them. "Hang out with your teammates for once."

Ian reluctantly went along.

Nobody was there. The pizza and Cokes were on a table. Ian scooped up a slice of lukewarm pepperoni and sausage pizza. He also grabbed a Coke that was sitting in ice. He knew they shouldn't be in the teacher's lounge, so he ate quickly.

Ian was about done with his slice of pizza when he started on his Coke. Steve and Andre had both polished off another piece.

"Let's go," Steve said. He moved toward the door that led into the cafeteria.

The cafeteria.

Where Davey was.

"I'm going this way," Ian stated.

He started to go out the way they had come in. But standing a few feet from the door were two teachers. He didn't have them for any classes, but he'd seen them around campus. Ian knew they could get him in trouble. If he got caught in the teacher's lounge eating their food, he would be toast.

"Why'd they have to talk right here?" Ian wondered.

He quickly went back into the lounge.

"What's up?" Steve asked. Ian didn't realize Steve and Andre were following him.

"There are teachers out there," Ian said.

"That's why I wanted to go this way." Andre pointed to the door in the cafeteria.

"Unless you don't want to," Steve said.

"There are probably teachers in there too." Ian knew that was a lame excuse.

"It's packed with students. There's no way they're gonna notice us!" Andre said.

"I think he's scared, Andre." Steve shot Ian an icy glare.

"Me too." Andre now looked at Ian the same way.

"Scared? Scared of what?" Ian knew the answer. And he knew they were right.

"Your brother." Steve smiled.

Before Ian knew what happened, Andre and Steve pushed him through the door that led into the cafeteria.

It was the first time Ian had stepped foot in it during lunch since the school year started. It was filled with students. There were no teachers in sight. Right in front of Ian was Davey sitting with his classmates.

"Later," Steve laughed. He and Andre walked away, snickering as they left.

Ian turned. Before he knew what was happening, Davey, with a huge smile on his face, was walking over to him with his arms in the air. It was as if it had been years since Davey had seen his big brother.

The bruises on his face from Ian's punches were almost all gone. Davey never held a grudge. It was almost like it never happened.

Ian turned to leave the cafeteria, but it was too packed and he couldn't move fast enough. As some people brushed past Davey, Ian tried to get away. Ian knew he needed to be a lot quicker. Davey immediately picked up on Ian's body language.

Ian turned and saw his brother's smile fade into confusion, then a scowl.

If only Ian could get out of the cafeteria. Then he'd be safe.

"Ian! No, Ian! Nobody!" Davey shrieked through the din.

Ian watched as Davey suddenly grabbed one of the students walking between them and tried to bite him on the shoulder.

"Argh! *What the hell!*" the student screamed. He whipped around and faced

Davey. For a second, Ian thought Davey was going down. Ian started to move toward them. He was going to try and get between them if he could. Davey lunged. Ian was going to be too late.

Out of nowhere, Greg appeared and wrapped Davey in a bear hug. In seconds they were on the ground. Davey was kicking and screaming. Even in the loud cafeteria, he could be heard over everything. He tried to break the bear hug. He tried to bite Greg's arms. He was kicking. Davey was trying anything to fight back.

As quickly as it started, Greg had contained Davey in a position where he was on his stomach. Greg had Davey's arms pinned to the ground with his knees as he sat on Davey's back.

School security rushed into the cafeteria and cleared out the other students. The bell rang, signaling that lunch was over. Everybody headed back to class. Ian, just like before, blended in with them and went back to class as well.

As he sat in computer science, he didn't feel any guilt for not helping his brother. Ian had bigger concerns. Like the future.

Davey had been getting into trouble since he started going to school, but he never faced any serious consequences. He just seemed to do bad stuff. He'd lose privileges or activities that he was look-ing forward to doing, but he never got into *real* trouble. What if Davey did something really bad to someone ten years from now? Would he go to jail?

Where was Davey going to go after high school? Would he get a job? Ian had heard his mom talk about some program that placed people with special needs in jobs. Could Davey do that? Could he work? What about when Davey got really old? What if he got sick? His mom was barely making enough money now. She wasn't going to live forever. Who would take care of Davey once she was gone? Would Ian be responsible for him?

Ian realized that no matter what happened in his future, Davey would always be a part of it.

More Bad News

We always look for ways to strengthen the rosters midseason," Coach Banks was saying. Ian wasn't really listening.

He just knew he wasn't going to be on the varsity team any longer.

"Rather than have you ride the bench for varsity, I'd rather put you back on JV where you'll get all the field time you can handle. And they could *really* use the help. You'll definitely be on varsity next year."

Coach Banks continued to talk. Ian couldn't listen.

"You'll suit up for the next varsity game but be back on JV after that."

Ian wanted to defend himself. He wanted to stand up and scream that Coach Banks had put him on varsity for a reason. That he deserved to be there. That it wasn't his fault that the team hated him because of Steve.

But Ian didn't say anything.

"You're a really talented player, Ian. I've enjoyed having you on the team." Coach Banks smiled.

And with that Ian was off to the locker room to suit up for one of the last varsity practices of his sophomore year. He was back on JV.

So much for Coach Banks's words that Ian was going to be a varsity man for the rest of his high school career. Ian wasn't surprised. After his parents divorced, he stopped trusting adults.

Ian sat in front of his open locker, staring at his varsity uniform. It wasn't much different from the junior varsity uniform—except the JV uniform held a lot less status in school.

He could feel himself starting to tear up. Ian did his best to hold them back. This only made matters worse. He was happy the team was on the field. It was humiliating enough being cut from varsity. Ian didn't want anybody to know he had cried about it.

Then he started thinking about all the things he didn't want people to know about. Davey. Autism. Home. His disengaged father. The demotion to JV.

The tears were really starting to flow.

Just as quickly, Ian pulled himself together. He grabbed a towel from his locker. Wiped his eyes. He was ready to move on.

Ian Taylor wasn't used to all this self pity. He didn't have time for it. He had too many other responsibilities. He quickly suited up and went out to practice.

Another Weekend at Dad's

Davey was watching YouTube on the iPad while an endless supply of cartoons spewed out of the 60-inch flat-screen TV at his dad's.

He sat on the couch. Ian sat across from him in a reclining chair. He half thought about reclining all the way back and going to sleep. He was so bored. Instead he got up and walked out of the media room to look for his father. Ian had a lot on his mind. He wanted to talk with someone. Anyone.

Ian's dad's house was huge. It completely dwarfed the house that Ian, Davey, and his mom rented. It had many bedrooms, a long, winding staircase, and a luxurious pool out back.

Ian's house didn't. He had overheard Melissa tell a friend that Ian's dad and Amy had pooled their money and bought this place. It was going to be for *their* family. Ian was really glad Amy wasn't there that weekend. She had some high-paying job and was out of town.

He found his dad in the kitchen, working on his laptop.

"You guys okay?" Ian's dad asked. He was entranced by whatever he was doing on the computer.

"Yeah," Ian said. "Davey's fine."

"Good. Good." His dad continued staring at the computer screen as he talked.

"You busy with the wedding?" Ian asked.

"Busy isn't the word."

Ian had been in the room almost a minute. His dad still hadn't looked at him.

"Dad," Ian started, "do you ever keep secrets from people?"

"Yeah, sometimes."

"Why? Is it about really important stuff?" Ian started to pull a chair out so he could sit down.

"Well, sometimes." His dad looked at him for the first time since he came into the kitchen.

Before Ian's dad could say another word, his cell phone rang. He picked it up.

"Hey, Amy," he said quickly. "… I've been trying to. I just can't find that e-mail with the quote."

Ian's dad repositioned himself in front of the computer again. He was done with this conversation. Ian had been dismissed.

Ian stopped pulling out the chair. He knew it was a waste of time to sit down.

He walked out of the kitchen. His dad didn't even notice.

Ian's dad also didn't notice when Ian walked out of the house.

Lost in LA

It only took a few minutes for Ian to realize that he had no idea where he was going. In fact, it wasn't long before Ian had walked out of Brentwood, where his father lived. He soon found himself walking past tall skyscrapers, kids on the street, hipsters at cafes—the melting pot that was Los Angeles.

Ian told himself he'd stop walking when he felt like it. But he didn't feel like it. He wanted to be lost in the city. To have no more worries about his life. To just survive. Out here he figured he could live in the moment. That suited him just fine.

He wondered if people might worry about him … if his dad even knew he was gone.

Ian walked for a while. In the back of his head, he figured that he would eventually circle back to his dad's. After circling a few times, Ian had to accept that he was lost.

Still, he didn't care. He had his cell phone on him. He could always call someone if he needed help. Ian didn't want to go back to his dad's house. Not right now. He didn't think he could take it. If he had to spend another Saturday with his dad ignoring them, and Davey sitting in front of the TV watching *Garfield* or something, he was going to go crazy.

Ian was starting to get mad all over again. He didn't want to go home angry. He didn't want to go home at all.

He was so wrapped up in his thoughts that he didn't notice them.

CHAPTER 34

Out of His Element

Yo, white boy, you belong north of Pico,"
the smallest of the three big guys said.
They laughed at Ian. They were all Latino.
Two of them had small mustaches. They
wore baggy pants, clean white tank tops,
and dark blue knit caps. They couldn't
have been much older than Ian, but they
were old enough.

Ian may have been a big deal on the
football field: But he knew he wasn't anything here.

Ian stared at them. He was still angry, but he didn't want to say the wrong thing. He knew these guys were looking for any reason to beat him up.

"Is he gonna cry?" one of them asked.

"No," Ian said. His anger was starting to be replaced by fear. He thought things were bad before; now he knew they could get a whole lot worse.

"I think he is," the biggest one said.

Ian stared at the ground. He wanted to buy some time. Maybe somebody would come along and help him. Maybe his father. Maybe Davey. But Ian knew that wasn't going to happen. Ever.

"Let's give him a little help," the smallest one said.

Before Ian knew what was happening, the guys started reigning punches and kicks on him. Using his football skills, he covered up well, but the blows still hit hard. Ian was able to pivot, and he turned himself away from them. He felt himself brush up against the biggest kid.

Because Ian had run so many football plays in his life, he could feel the movement of his attackers and anticipate where they were trying to grab or kick him.

The biggest kid reached for Ian, but Ian was too fast. He managed to grab the kid's shirt. Using all of his strength, he spun around and threw the big guy into the other two. They didn't fall down, but the seconds they needed to regain their balance gave Ian more than enough time to get away.

He had never run this fast in his life. And that included at a football game. Ian moved past people on the street. He didn't stop at crosswalks. He even dodged a few cars at some intersections. He didn't slow down until it was almost impossible to keep going.

By the time he stopped, he realized that he was even more lost. Ian took out his cell phone but he didn't call anybody. He didn't want to call his dad or his mom and ask for help. He didn't think he'd been gone long enough for anybody to care or notice. Ian put his cell phone back in his pocket.

He looked around at the street signs to see if any of them looked familiar. They didn't.

His cell phone rang.

CHAPTER 35

Jessica to the Rescue

Ian saw Jessica's ID on the phone. For a second he thought about not answering it. Then he did.

"Hey," Ian said quickly.

"What's up?" Jessica's voice was as enthusiastic as always. Not a care in the world. Ian already knew it was a mistake answering his phone.

"I'm in LA."

"You are?"

"Yeah, I thought I told you. This is my dad's weekend."

"Oh." Jessica seemed upset. Ian hadn't told her and he knew it. He remembered this was weekend they were supposed to spend a day together. "Where are you?" she asked.

"I don't know." He looked around after he said that. Nothing looked familiar.

"What?" she questioned.

"I don't know." His tone was harsher.

"Are you mad?"

Ian wanted to go off. He wanted to tell Jessica everything. But he couldn't. He had to keep up his lie. His facade. Even if it was crashing down around him. Even if he knew she knew the truth and wasn't saying anything.

"I bailed at my dad's house. I'm in LA. I don't know where I am," he finally said.

"Why? What's going on?" She seemed genuinely concerned.

"Forget it. I'll call you later—"

"What?! Why are you hanging up?

You're lost." Jessica sounded angry. Ian was dying to disconnect the call. "What're your cross streets?"

"Why? Are you gonna come and get me?" He almost wanted to laugh, but he was too angry and anxious.

"Yes." Jessica's tone was definitive. "I came up to LA today with my parents. They're visiting some friends, and they let me take the car to the Grove. Just tell me where you are. I'll put it in the nav and come get you."

"I'm probably really far from you …" Seeing Jessica now was the last thing he wanted.

"I don't care. I'm coming to get you. What're your cross streets? I'm not gonna leave you in LA when you don't know where you are. Believe it or not, I care about you, Ian."

Those words were the ones he had been waiting to hear from his parents, from other members of his family. From anybody who knew his situation.

But Jessica said them first. Jessica. The girl he'd held at arm's length. He'd hidden his true self from her. He hadn't wanted her to get too close. Too intimate. He was just like his mother, pushing people away.

Ian looked around and told her his cross streets.

CHAPTER 36

What Are
Friends For?

Watching Jessica pull up made Ian feel even worse. First because it was such a nice car, and second because he wouldn't be in driver's education until next semester. Even when he could drive, he'd be at the mercy of his mom's Honda, which wasn't nearly as cool as Jessica's car. Jessica looked perfect in her parents' car. Someone like her belonged in it. Not Ian.

Ian got in the car and they started driving. The air conditioning was on. The entire car smelled nice, and the seats were the most comfortable ones Ian had ever felt. The front display looked like something out of a movie. Ian stared at the road ahead.

"You'll have to tell me where I'm going—" Jessica started.

"My dad lives off Brentwood Boulevard and Grant Street," he cut her off.

"What happened to your face?"

"I was born with it," Ian snapped back. It was meant to be a joke, but Jessica didn't laugh. "I went for a walk and got lost. I ran into some guys who didn't like me." Ian had yet to look at her since he got in the car. He could feel Jessica's eyes on him.

"On the phone you said you left your dad's house—"

"Do we have to keep talking about it?" Ian barked. His face was starting to hurt.

"Yes! We have to talk about it. We never talk about anything important." She was starting to get mad.

"We talk about football and cheerleading. Isn't that good enough?" Ian hated trying to hurt her but he had to keep her away. He had to …

"What does that mean? Does this have anything to do with your brother, Davey?"

Ian met Jessica's eyes for the first time. He didn't know what to say.

She knew about Davey. He knew deep down that she knew. But there was always a tiny doubt. Now there was none. She knew that the boy who screamed, cried, attacked people, acted like a baby … she knew that he was Ian's brother.

"What do you care? You laughed at him when Jeff imitated Davey at that party. You probably laugh at me behind my back. You're probably still with Steve, and I'm just a joke in your perfect world!" Ian was seething. He had longed to let out his real feelings. The only problem was he didn't feel good about it at all.

"How can you say that?" Jessica's tone was measured. "All I've ever been is nice to you, Ian. I'm sorry about laughing, but I didn't know Jeff was making fun of Davey. I shouldn't have laughed anyway. It was stupid and I'm stupid sometimes. Sorry. But the only thing I'm really guilty of is trying to get to know you!"

They stared at one another. Ian opened up his mouth.

"Why would I date you just to make fun of you?" she asked. "Do you understand how lame that is? I wouldn't go out with somebody, even as friends, if I didn't care about them. If anybody acts like they don't care, it's you. You're always making excuses. Trying to hide your family... never telling me anything. I really like you, Ian." She went on, "Why wouldn't I like Davey too? How can I know what you're feeling about anything if you don't talk to me?"

Ian didn't know what to say. Jessica had just said everything he hadn't been able to express.

"And as for Steve ... we're done. We're still friends but we're not together. Do you know why he hasn't played much this year?"

"He's probably getting ready for college—" Ian began.

"No," Jessica's tone had softened just a little. "It's because his dad has advanced Parkinson's disease. Steve has to help out more at home and at his dad's business. He might not even start college next year."

Ian couldn't believe it. Steve Morgan. This person who seemed to have the perfect life, who laughed at people who were different, who picked on Ian ... he was dealing with something very similar.

"Pull the car over," Ian said.

"Why? You're not getting out."

"Just pull it over, please."

Jessica eyed him as she pulled the car over to the curb.

And there in the middle of Saturday afternoon LA traffic, Ian proceeded to spill his guts. He told Jessica all about Davey. How for his whole life everything had been about Davey. He told her about his mom, his dad. About football. He told her it was the only thing he'd ever been really good at. How he was counting on football to pay for college. Ian told her how he wanted to go far away from everything and everyone.

"Even me?" she asked. Her eyes had that look that melted his heart a million times before.

"No," Ian said. "I like you so much, Jessica. I've been so scared that if you knew the truth about me … if I was anything but this star on the football field, you wouldn't like me."

"Ian,"—Jessica took his hand in hers—"I wanna know everything. You should feel like you can tell me anything. I'm your girlfriend, aren't I?"

They kissed, and it was better than it had ever been. It was official. Jessica considered herself to be Ian's girlfriend.

Later, when Jessica dropped him off at his dad's house, he'd felt something he hadn't felt since they'd started dating. That afternoon Jessica had become more than someone he was dating, even more than a just a girlfriend to Ian.

She was his friend as well.

For the first time in his life, Ian felt like he really had somebody in his corner. Somebody who *wanted* to be by his side.

CHAPTER 37

The Next Morning

Ian's dad hadn't notice that he'd left. Then he saw the bruises on Ian's face and arms.

"I went for a run and fell down," Ian had told him. His dad didn't ask any questions.

This was the same story he told his mom when he spoke to her on the phone Sunday morning. He also told her he ended up hanging out with Jessica because she was in LA too.

When Ian was done talking to Melissa, he went into the room where Davey was watching TV. The iPad was next to him, but he was more focused on the *Snow White* DVD that his dad had put on. Davey was doing the things he always he did. Staring intently at the screen, slapping his hands against his legs and squeezing them … he'd seen this movie a million times, but it was like he was seeing it for the first time.

Ian sat down next to him.

Davey, never taking his eyes off the screen, put his hand on Ian's shoulder to reassure himself somehow. Ian stared at his brother, who seemed unaware that he was being watched.

"I can't focus on anything the way you can focus on movies," Ian said aloud. If Davey heard him, he didn't acknowledge what Ian said. The only thing that came close to holding his attention like that was football.

And Jessica.

Davey started to laugh at something on the screen. His smile made Ian smile. Ian grabbed his brother and tickled his stomach. This made Davey laugh even more, but he still didn't look at Ian. He laughed like this was the best time he had ever had in his life. Ian loved it when Davey laughed like this. Ian loved when his brother was happy.

If only he could be happy all of the time.

Ian gave Davey some sensory squeezes on his arms and shoulders. Davey liked those as well.

Back at School

That Monday morning Ian slept in and got to school late. He arrived at about the same time as the buses were showing up.

Davey and Greg got off their bus. Greg had been riding with Davey for a while. He didn't used to do that, but things changed when Davey hit his head against the window the year before.

The front of the school was filled with people. It seemed as if everybody who went to Davis was out there.

Ian saw that Davey saw him. There was distance between them. Like before, Ian could've easily blended in with the crowd. This time he chose not to. He walked over to Davey.

"What's up, Davey?" Ian gave his brother a high five.

Davey tried to hang on Ian a little bit, like he did at home, but Ian moved so they would look like two normal high school kids talking.

"This okay?" Greg asked.

"Yeah." Ian nodded his head. "It's fine."

Ian felt like all the eyes at Davis High School were on him. But they weren't, and he knew it.

And even if they were ... he didn't care. At least not as much anymore.

Blind Eye

Ian and Jessica walked through the campus together holding hands. Even though they had kissed, there was something about holding hands with Jessica that superseded everything. Ever since the talk in the car, they were officially boyfriend and girlfriend.

Ian's happiness also might've had something to do with him not hiding anything anymore. He no longer felt the need to watch his back. He didn't need to think three steps ahead so he could avoid Davey around every corner.

Deep down, Ian had known he wouldn't

be able to keep up the secret forever. He had been mortified at the thought of people knowing the truth about him and Davey. However, he had no idea how good it would feel to no longer carry that burden.

"Are you busy Saturday?" Ian asked Jessica.

"You can't see me on Friday?" Jessica sounded bummed.

"I was thinking we could do something both days."

Jessica looked at him and smiled.

"Two days of hanging out together. Sounds pretty serious, Ian."

"It is."

They kissed briefly.

As they pulled away, Ian saw Davey and Greg in the distance.

Ian and Jessica passed some guys on varsity. Ian didn't know them well. They were seniors. Now with him going back to JV, he probably never would.

"Look at the way he walks!" he overheard one of them say. They all cracked up.

Ian's heart sank.

There was nobody else around, and unless the guys on the team were making fun of Greg, they had to be talking about Davey.

Ian could hear them continue to laugh. Jessica was talking, but Ian didn't hear a word she said. He was too angry.

Eventually, Greg and Davey were out of sight. Ian and Jessica were too far away from the guys who were laughing and talking smack for him to say anything.

He hated those guys for making fun of Davey. But he hated himself more for not confronting them.

Not Letting It Slide

Later that day, Ian wasn't himself at his final varsity practice of his sophomore year. He was so out of it that he missed a pass he easily should've caught.

Ian could feel all eyes on him. They were probably happy he wasn't going to be on varsity anymore. There hadn't been a big announcement or anything, but everybody seemed to know. Shawn and Ryan from his JV team told him how stoked they were that he was coming back. Jessica said he was too good for this year's varsity team. Ian was bummed, but he wasn't going to miss these guys at all. They hadn't ever accepted him and probably never would.

Coach Banks was having both Ian and Steve run plays, even though Ian wasn't going to play the last game. Ian picked up the ball he'd missed off the ground.

"Nice catch," Steve said. "If you're special ed."

Andre, Jeff, and some of the other guys nearby laughed at Ian.

"Yeah," Ian said. "You're one to laugh."

Steve's expression instantly changed. The way their eyes met signaled that they both knew what Ian meant.

Before Ian knew what happened, Steve was in his face. The other team members circled them.

This was the confrontation they had been waiting for.

"Let's go!" Steve growled.

He pushed Ian. Ian pushed him right back.

Steve moved to throw a punch. Ian ducked and rushed him. He wrapped his arms around Steve's waist and took him to the ground. They rolled around a bit. Ian didn't want to fight Steve, he just wanted to contain him. To let him know that if he or anybody else was going to make fun of Davey, they'd better be ready to fight.

Eventually, Steve's size was too much. He got on top of Ian and started wailing on him. Ian did his best to cover up, but a few punches got in. They didn't hurt, but that was probably because Ian was covered in a helmet and other padding.

"What the hell are you guys doing?" Coach Banks broke through all the players and pulled Steve off of Ian.

Steve was still seething.

Ian quickly got up off the ground. His nose was bleeding.

"He started it, Coach. He made fun of—" Steve began.

"What are you? A bunch of sissies? Don't give me any of that cry baby crap!" Coach Banks furiously cut him off. "You and this whole team have been riding Ian the entire season. All he's wanted to do is help this football team."

Coach Banks looked at all the players. Only Ian met his gaze. Then Coach got in Steve's face.

"What kind of man makes fun of somebody with special needs?" He was now inches from Steve's nose. "Especially when they know something about it?"

Coach Banks looked at everybody on the team again.

"What kind of men are you anyway?" He eyed Ian. "Taylor has more inner strength than all of you put together. He's had to shoulder a bigger burden than most of you could ever imagine."

Coach Banks looked at all the players. They were looking at him now.

"Now let's stop fighting with each other and get in formation for our game against Bay View tomorrow. I can guarantee you, they're gonna bring it!"

Everybody did as they were told. Ian started to walk off the field so Steve could take his spot.

"Morgan, hit the bench," Coach Banks said.

Ian turned around.

"What? But, Coach, he—" Steve said incredulously.

"You heard me. This season's still got a few more games for you to play. Taylor's gonna play his last one on this team." Coach Banks eyed Ian.

It seemed like Coach Banks was smiling. Ian didn't want to stare at him for too long. He might change his mind.

Steve angrily took off his helmet and stormed away.

Ian got in his position. The play was run and he took off down the field. He was excited to be playing his final game. More importantly, he was happy that everything about Davey was really out in the open at Davis High School now.

No more hiding. No more pretending to be somebody he wasn't.

CHAPTER 41
Final Game

Davis was down by three against Bay View High School. There were only two minutes left in the game. Steve was switching off between sitting on the bench and standing up. He was yelling plays too. He may not have been playing, but that didn't mean he wanted Davis to lose.

When he could, Ian looked at Melissa in the stands with Davey. He was watching something on the DVD player again. Every so often, he would shake and clench his teeth. He looked like he was in pain, but Ian knew better. He knew his brother was just going through something in his head.

"I wish I knew what he's feeling. If he's feeling anything at all," Ian mused. Ian didn't know. His mom didn't know. Nobody knew. The best they could do was help Davey through it.

Sitting with Melissa and Davey was Todd. He had broken up with Ian's mom, but apparently they talked it out and had gotten back together. Ian loved his mom. If she couldn't be with his dad, he wanted her to be with somebody she cared about. And who cared about her.

"You just need be more open, Mom. Like I'm learning to be," he thought.

Ian watched as Jessica and the other cheerleaders ran through a cheer. She did everything one hundred percent. Her eyes, smile, and spirit were so big. Ian felt like if he closed his eyes and waited, all he would hear was her.

Ian and the rest of the players moved into formation.

"This game is gonna be over soon. Next week I'll be back on junior varsity. Who cares? I did the best I could for these guys," Ian thought.

Ian still wanted to win tonight. He always wanted to win.

This was why when the play was called, Ian took off down the field as fast as he possibly could. He felt as good now as he had when the game started. "I'm not leaving anything on the field," he kept telling himself.

Ian turned and saw Carlos trying to assess his passing options. The Bay View offense was closing in fast. Carlos seemed to look at Ian. He was wide open but Carlos still didn't want to throw the ball to him. It quickly became clear that Ian was his only option.

Carlos threw the ball in the air.

Just like in a movie, everything moved in slow motion for Ian. The crowd got quiet. He could feel himself breathing. Everything in the world seemed to stop as Ian waited for the ball.

"Relax," he told himself. "Keep it steady. This won't be like your first game with Jones. You got this."

With complete ease, the ball fell into Ian's hands. And then, like he had so many times before, Ian tore down the field and made a touchdown.

This was what Ian Taylor did. He played football. He cared for his brother. He helped his mom. He got things done.

Time may have slowed down but the clock didn't. It quickly ran out.

All the Davis players ran over to congratulate him. Steve, Andre, and Jeff were with them.

The game was over and Davis High School had won.

And Ian was a big part of that.

CHAPTER 42

The Introduction

Even in the cold night air, Jessica's lips felt good. He held her close to him as they hugged.

"Thank you," Ian whispered.

"For what?" she giggled.

"For everything." He smiled. Ian kissed her again.

"Is your mom here?" Jessica beamed.

Ian took her hand and led her over to where his mom, Davey, and Todd were standing.

Ian knew he'd better talk with them first. The game was over and Davey wouldn't want to hang around.

"Mom, this is Jessica," Ian said.

"It's great to meet you," Jessica said. She extended her hand and Melissa shook it warmly.

"It's great to meet you too." Melissa smiled. "Ian's got good taste."

"Thank you." Jessica blushed.

"I'm Todd," Todd said. He put his arm around Melissa. There was a time when it might've bothered Ian. It didn't anymore. Todd was all right. Even if he did try too hard sometimes.

"This is my guy." Melissa put her arm around Todd's waist. "Well, one of my guys."

All the attention seemed to turn to Davey.

"Davey," Ian started. "Can you …"

"Hi, Jessica," Davey said shyly. He didn't make eye contact with her, and even though it was hard for him to greet her,

Davey had done it. Without any prompting, without any of the usual things that people had to do for him, he said hi to Ian's girlfriend.

Ian smiled and gave Davey a hug. He hugged Ian back.

Ian still felt embarrassed by his brother. However, he also knew that the more he embraced who (and how) Davey was, the more comfortable he would become.

Ian decided not to think about any of that tonight. Things were good now and that was what mattered.

Back at It

The bell rang and school let out for the day.

Ian stood with Shawn, Ryan, and some other members of the JV squad. They were all suited up and stretching before practice.

Ian had expected to feel weird being back on the team, but he didn't. The junior varsity squad had only won two games the whole season. Coach Geary had personally told Ian he expected him to help change that.

"You miss varsity?" Shawn asked.

"I don't know," Ian said. "I just got back."

He looked around at the junior varsity cheerleaders. He was going to miss not seeing Jessica at practice. Then Ian remembered he was going to see her later that night.

"He just misses being around his girlfriend," Ryan teased. Then he laughed. It was like he was reading Ian's mind.

Ian smiled. Since he had made it official with Jessica, everyone knew they were together.

"Can you blame him?" Tyler asked. Ian didn't know Tyler well, but he was thankful for the compliment.

Someone shrieked. Ian knew it was Davey before the other guys knew who it was.

Ian glanced over at the bus area across from the field. He saw that Davey was screaming at Greg. He even hit him. Greg easily turned Davey and redirected him. They kept walking over to the buses.

Davey screamed a little bit more but eventually stopped.

"Who is that guy?" Tyler asked. He turned back to Ian, Shawn, and Ryan.

They put their heads down and eyed Ian sheepishly. This didn't bother Ian as much as he thought it might. He stared Tyler directly in the eye.

"That is my brother," Ian stated.

Tyler stared at Ian. He didn't seem to know if he was being serious.

"Really?"

"Yeah. His name is Davey."

"All right, guys! Bring it in. Come on, get to it. Hustle!" Coach Geary yelled as he walked out onto the field.

Ian smiled at Shawn, Ryan, and Tyler.

"Let's go!" he said, then ran off toward Coach Geary. They all followed him.

Ian had a feeling that his life was not only going to be better now, but easier as well.

Here, Evan is recording a voice for his animated horror film, Insect.

ABOUT THE AUTHOR

Evan Jacobs was born in Long Island,
New York. His family moved to California
when he was four years old. They settled
in Fountain Valley, where he still lives
today.

As a filmmaker, Evan has directed
eleven low-budget films. He has also had

various screenplays produced and realized by other directors. He co-wrote the film *Knockout*, starring "Stone Cold" Steve Austin. He co-authored the thriller *Distant Shore*. He is currently juggling several movie and book projects.

Evan is also a behavior interventionist for people who have special needs. He works with a variety of students to make their days as successful as possible. *Screaming Quietly* is his third young adult novel. You can find out more about him at www.anhedeniafilms.blogspot.com.